JACK AT DEATH'S DOOR

A Jack of All Trades novel

DH Smith

Earlham Books

Published 2018 by Earlham Books
Book design & cover art by Lia at Free Your Words
(*www.FreeYourWords.com*)

ISBN: 978-1-909804-30-2

Author's Note

The cemetery in this novel is something like Manor Park cemetery but with major differences. The flower stall is in a different place, I have moved a cemetery road, moved a mausoleum and made a total change of ownership. The current owners of Manor Park Cemetery bear no relationship to my quarrelling family. Fiction takes liberties. For the above reasons I have called the cemetery in this novel Forest Gate Cemetery.

PART ONE:
THE CAST AND SETTING

Chapter 1

Jack drove slowly through the wrought-iron gates. The thick pillars on either side had church steeple tops. He stopped ten yards further on, outside the cemetery office, a stout, grey stone, single storey building. A serious edifice to deal with the serious business of disposing of the dead. Jack didn't feel altogether comfortable working in a cemetery, having absorbed the superstitions associated with coffins, bones and graveyards. He only ever came here for funerals. The grounds had a solemnity, a sadness, mingled with the awareness of his own mortality and fear of what was underground. But it was daytime, and ghosts strolled after dark. Work was work, and he needed it. The van needed repairing, the maintenance he was paying Alison for his daughter, Mia, would drain his account this month. There was the mortgage coming up. He'd work in hell if he was paid in advance.

Jack leaned back in his van and rubbed his eyes. He hadn't slept well, but employment had got him out of bed. His obligation was to do X so he could get paid Y, in order to pass it on to A, B and C. Grubby lucre, going in and out of the bank, who assured him in their ads he was their only purpose on earth. But wouldn't give him a loan. Probably just as well, as he'd have to pay it back and have even less money in the months to come.

Ring a ring of roses, pass the greasy notes.

He was in a grim mood. The trick was to get working, to forget the nexus of obligations. Engage with saw and hammer, create order from timber, brick and nails. The beginning was the leap, to make purpose out of a meagre fuel of a slice of toast and a cup of tea. He must make the first steps. Talk to the man. Look like a builder in control of tools and materials who knew exactly where to cut the wood and how to lay concrete.

Maria had pulled the rug from under him yesterday evening. He'd just showered to go out to dinner with her, when her text came.

'It's not working, Jack. I was going to tell you over dinner, but why waste money on good food? Sorry to do it this way, but I don't like scenes.'

He'd considered phoning her, but what was there to say? You can't persuade someone the relationship is working when they have just told you it isn't. But it did empty the world of meaning, of solid purpose.

So make some. He rolled his shoulders. He was alive, he was sober. Cut your losses, even if you've lost sleep. These things happen, he told himself. Not everyone is for everyone. Horses for courses and other truisms.

Work. Saw, hammer. Who needs love?

Mist was circling the gravestones, a chill in the air. Another month or so and it would be dark when he left home in the mornings. He rubbed his hands together, the van had hardly warmed up in the short drive over. At least it was a local job, making the best of his time. The sky was overcast like a dirty sheet. It might rain later.

The day had barely begun but felt ancient, as his sleep had been so fractured. How did other people manage? Getting up every morning, all weathers, catching the train to work. Fear and duty; the twin whips across the shoulders. Move, Jack, and once you are moving – keep in motion like a planet revolving round its sun.

Tomorrow is another day.

Where was the comfort in that? It didn't say whether tomorrow would be better or worse. Or whether you'd still be alive even, though if you were dead then all your troubles would die with you. Your debts, your loves, your lack of loves, all the necessities flashed away when life switched off.

Jack leaped out of the van as if in panic. No more of this. He closed the van and strode forward, propelling his body in the hope of propelling his mind into other tracks. He pushed open the door of the cemetery office. Confront the human; say to him what you have to say, and even on a cold, misty morning, you might convince yourself you are better than you are.

'Wondered if you were coming in or not,' said a man across the deep brown, shiny counter.

The office was half panelled in dark wood. The cream walls above had framed photos of the cemetery, early ones in black and white, later ones in colour, showing the seasons and the changes in the cemetery layout. A woman in a corner was typing and gazing into a screen, her desk the brown of the panelling as if they'd had a job lot of deep brown stained timber.

The man who had spoken was in brown too, as if to merge with the surroundings. The jacket of his suit was unbuttoned and his brick-red tie flapped against the shirt like an exhausted fish. He was clean shaven with a bulbous nose, his hair wiry and greying.

'I was having a think,' said Jack, 'sorting myself out.' He attempted a smile, to be affable as he indicated his van through the window. 'Where to start and all that.'

'Let's get this clear,' said the man, his eyes widening as he spoke, 'you are here on sufferance.'

Jack bridled, instantly alert.

'I'm sorry,' he said, taking care to remain polite, 'but I've work to do here.' He searched in his overall pockets for the letter of instructions.

'Jack of All Trades,' sneered the man, looking out the window at the van and its catchwords painted on the side.

He had immaculate teeth, like a portcullis. 'I've seen you around. A man about town.'

'It's been arranged,' insisted Jack. 'I was here with Mrs Little on Friday. She said everything had been agreed with the cemetery.' He held out the screwed up letter. 'Here's my instructions.'

The man brushed it away. 'I know what it says. The letter is copied in to me, you might have noted.'

The woman at the computer had stopped typing. She was obviously listening in, without looking their way, pretending to be reading the screen.

Jack glanced at the letter and found the name of the man. 'I'm not here to cause trouble, Mr Coe. I'm just a workman going about his business. I came into your office, so you'd know who I was and what I was doing.'

'I know what you're doing,' exclaimed Coe, leaning forward on the counter, 'and I wish I didn't.' He stood upright. 'Let's keep this short. Here's the rules. Keep out of my way, number one, two and three. You can come in and out with your van to drop off materials, but you can't park here.'

'You've a works car park at the back,' exclaimed Jack. 'I was told I could use it.'

'You can come in and out with your van to drop off materials, but you can't park here,' repeated the man, as if Jack hadn't heard him the first time. 'If there's a funeral nearby, stop working. No swearing, no singing, no banter, no music. When you leave your job, even for a short period, fence it off.'

'What about toilet access?'

'It's for permanent staff only.'

Jack took a breath, wondering how to reply, catching sight of himself in the oval mirror across the counter. Against the light from the window, he was a silhouette, curly hair showing, with just a little light catching in his eyes.

'Mr Coe,' he said, holding up his hands in a placatory fashion, 'I'm only here to work. I won't be any hassle.'

'Your presence is a hassle.' Coe turned his back and strode across the office. He pushed open a door and went in to a back room, slamming the door behind him.

Jack rubbed a hand through his hair, nonplussed. He'd thought it had all been settled. 'What was all that about?' he said to the woman.

She turned to him. She was perhaps mid 30s, with a full figure, her hair auburn and short. She put a finger to her lips and hissed, 'There's a toilet in the crematorium.'

'Thank you,' said Jack, picking up her whispered tone. 'Why all that from him?'

'Politics,' she said, indicating the closed door. 'I can't say any more,' adding as an afterthought, 'Sorry, but I want to keep my job.'

Jack nodded. 'I understand. And I just want to work.' He began to walk to the door, and then turned, 'Miss, Mrs...?'

'Maureen,' she said and smiled. 'Mrs.'

'Jack,' he said, pleased to be able to smile back.

Chapter 2

He drove sedately, keeping under the regulation five miles per hour, to keep the peace of the cemetery and to not give Coe any further grievance. Mrs Little, his client, had distinctly told him it was all sorted out. She had assured him. But then she wasn't working here. He thought of phoning her but what on earth would he say? *Mr Coe is giving me a hard time.* He hadn't forbidden Jack working here, simply made life difficult. Maureen had called it 'politics'. What on earth did that mean? Some wrangling on some committee? What did that have to do with his job?

Up by the crematorium, ahead of him, there were a number of cars along with men and women, predominantly in black funeral wear, watching a coffin being carried out of a hearse by men in black tail coats and top hats. Jack halted; funerals had right of way, he knew without being told by Coe. It was a matter of respect.

The mourners were black and white men and women, more black than white. Jack wondered who had died, and searched for clues in the floral tributes laid on the ground and against the wall of the building. One said Mum, others said Nan. A mother then who was also a grandmother, presumably a wife, a sister, an aunty, seeing all these people. He reflected on who might come to his funeral. His mother if someone told her, maybe his dad, his daughter Mia, her mother Alison, a few friends. Would he have a partner by then? By when? He couldn't imagine living to 90, but who could say? A fast car or cancer might cut him down anytime. Or he might shuffle on in bedroom slippers into his pensioned years.

Watching, he wondered whether the funeral was a cremation or a burial? Cremation was the cheaper option. Up in flames and maybe a memorial rose bush. But a grave required space, increasingly expensive, and money for digging, for a stone and engraving. Black families still tended to go for burials. Their tradition.

The building was churchlike, brick-walled with a tall, thin spire. Jack had been inside once for an aunt's funeral. There was a hall with pews, quite antiseptic with nothing on the walls, in order to fit all denominations and none. He recalled the coffin on its high stand, decorated with curtains like a four poster bed. At the end of the homily, double doors behind the coffin had opened, and the coffin slid along the bed and between the doors as the curtains slowly closed. Was there a lift to take the coffin down? Or a slide? Did the coffin go straight into the roaring oven in the basement?

A few of the mourners were looking his way. An elderly black woman screwed up her face at the sight of a builder's van, as if he should have covered it in a black drape. He could have halted further back, but had been mid conversation with Mr Coe. And getting the better of him, once out of his presence.

The mourners were going inside. An elderly woman was weeping, a handkerchief pressed to her eyes. A middle-aged woman had her arm over her shoulder. He guessed sister and niece of the deceased. There were a scattering of children in Sunday best. One little boy, about five or six, was squirming in his shirt collar. Jack sympathised; he hated suits. And a tie was simply a colourful noose.

Once most were inside, he drove past the building and the flowers along the wall. He took a side road, the cambered surface a scattering of leaves and conkers, some still in their spiked green cases, others out and scattered, furniture brown with the split cases lying here and there.

The leaves were rolled and tanned like tobacco leaf. Jack was squeamish about crushing conkers. They'd been valuable barter in his childhood, playing conkers with the kids in the flats. But he was too old to get out and gather up the riches. Besides, kids didn't play conkers anymore. All into their tablets and smart phones.

Driving on, he winced as he bumped over the horse chestnuts, feeling the hiss as the yellow innards squeezed onto the road. Murder; how many corpses in his wake? Like Napoleon he didn't look back, but pressed on to Moscow, or rather to the cube of bricks in woven plastic at the edge of the roadway.

A squirrel raced across and leaped into a horse chestnut tree, and was out of sight. Did they eat conkers? He'd tried eating one as a child, and recalled spitting out the bitter flesh. Did horses eat them? Pigs did. They used to let them free in the forests. A great aunt had told him that during the war they'd roasted conkers to make coffee. Hard times can make you try anything.

He stopped the van and alighted by the cubical bag of bricks. Resting alongside were sacks of concrete mix and mortar. Jack took a brick from the pile. A beautiful red, almost apple colour. He wondered how the delivery driver had managed to get past Coe. Maybe Coe was in his back office doing whatever he did there. He couldn't imagine Coe getting in the cab and directing him. It would hurt him more than toothache.

Jack went to his van and pulled open the side door. He took out a wheelbarrow and the large square board he used for making concrete. Today, he'd lay the footings, the concrete foundation for the brickwork. It was only a low wall that he'd be building, so the footings needn't be deep, about four inches would do. A flat supporting surface to build up from. He'd considered buying cement, sand and aggregate in order to make up the concrete himself. But he'd end up with too much left over. If he had a yard it would be worth it, keeping what was over for another job, but all he had was a lock-up, so bags of concrete mix would serve.

After laying the concrete, the footings would be firm enough by tomorrow, so he could begin bricklaying. Three days' work in all, he'd estimated, weather permitting. Today the footings, tomorrow the bricklaying, the day after the paving stones and the woodwork. So much depended on the weather. The sky didn't look hopeful. The few blue lagoons were being squeezed out by clouds. All he could do was work on and hope he could get the concrete in before the deluge.

Jack loaded a sack of the mix into the wheelbarrow. On top he laid the mixing board, finding room for a spade, a shovel, his long spirit level, the float. Anything else? A bucket for water. He did a mental listing, making sure he had everything he needed, as he would have to move the van per Mr Coe's instructions.

Jack came off the roadway with the wheelbarrow and followed the bitumen path for 50 yards, about three quarters of the way to the site where he'd be working, grateful for its flat run, as the square board was tricky on top of the wheelbarrow, bouncing up and down once he left the level and was on the grass.

His site was marked out with four wooden tent pegs at each corner tied with string around the perimeter. This part of the cemetery had new graves. Some with a photo on the headstone, as had become the fashion. Much of the rest of the space was taken up with standard roses with memorial plaques at the foot. The nearest were about fifteen feet away from Jack's site. They would get closer over time, and then another space would be found to scatter the ashes and put the plaques.

He considered what he had to do. Remove the grass, down to soil, dig the shallow trench for the footings, then lay the concrete. Had he got everything out of the van? Coe wanted his van off site. A nuisance. The easiest thing would be to leave the van nearby, and then anything forgotten could be easily retrieved. But that was forbidden.

Leaving the wheelbarrow and contents, Jack started back to the van. Coe was no doubt in his office, watching and waiting for Jack to drive by. He stopped to consider. Should he leave the tools out while he drove off? Not a good idea. This was a stupid waste of time. He'd got them here but didn't want to risk losing them while he drove the van off. The wheelbarrow could stay, no one would take the board. But the float, the spade, the shovel, spirit level and bucket would have to go in the van. And then be brought back. What a pain!

Coe would be out of his office any minute, you could bet on it, ranting and raving, pointing at his watch. With his tools back in the van, Jack drove off, still fuming at the waste of effort. As he passed the hall, Jack saw the funeral procession heading away. They were following the hearse up one of the cemetery roads. It had to be a burial and the mourners were being led to the grave.

Which would he prefer? Quick flames or slow worms. Not much of a choice when it came to it. Rot or be grilled. A grave gave you a stone though, a few words to say you had existed once, more enduring than the plaques around the rose bushes.

Did that matter? Yes, no. He could argue it both ways.

He drove past Coe's office, purposely not looking in, and out through the main gates. The cemetery grounds were at the end of a cul-de-sac. There was a semi-circular area in front of the gates with no other vehicles present. Across the way was a stonemason's shop, from where could be heard the buzz of a grinder, a cloud of dust oozing from the entrance. Before getting out, Jack listed in his notebook what he'd need for today's work. This was so unnecessary. He'd done all this once. Spade, shovel, spirit level, float, bucket. Would he need anything else? It would be a chore to come outside again and get it.

Chapter 3

Jack locked his van and set off back. The spirit level, spade and shovel were over his shoulder, a black bucket containing the float dangling from his hand. As he passed the office, he again avoided eye contact with the enemy. It was then he recalled he didn't have his thermos of tea and lunch with him. How annoying. Should he go back to the van? Or sort it out when it came to his tea break in an hour or so. A little way ahead the flower stall was opening up. They could look after his tools for a minute while he went back to the van. Surely they'd be amenable.

A young woman was bringing out flowers from the shed on a trolley: cut flowers in vases, others in pots. He recognised roses and chrysanthemums. The others were familiar but he wasn't sure of the names.

'Are they pansies?' he said.

She smiled. 'Yes, they are.'

The woman was slim, wearing green dungarees over a pale blue blouse. She'd rolled up her sleeves. Her face was lightly freckled with a stub nose, her hair was straw coloured, wavy and untidy in a not unattractive way. She had a gap in her front teeth. But more importantly, she was friendly.

Jack said carefully, 'How do you get on with Mr Coe?'

She laughed, bringing her hand to her mouth to cover up the gap, but knew it was too late and she had gone red.

'I'm having a bridge put in tomorrow,' she said. 'I feel so self conscious.'

'Perfect teeth are boring,' said Jack.

'Yours aren't bad,' she said. 'They all yours?'

Jack laughed. 'A couple missing at the back. No one can see the gaps except a dentist.'

'Don't remind me of dentists,' she said, waving her hands to ward off the thought. 'You were asking about Mr Coe. Why, may I ask?'

'He doesn't want me here. He doesn't want my van here. What was the word he used? Under sufferance. He'd like me to disappear in a puff of smoke. Cremated.'

'He's my uncle,' she said.

'Ah,' said Jack carefully.

'He does play God,' she said. 'Thinks he owns the place as he's chair of the board. Though that might be coming to an end. There's a meeting this afternoon.' She held up a hand. 'I'd better not say any more.'

'I'm hardly likely to tell him.'

She smiled. Her hand hesitated at her mouth and gave up. 'It's mostly family, the board.' She shook her head. 'It's going to be an awful meeting.'

'Nothing like families for rows,' said Jack.

She indicated the office with her head. 'I bet he's watching us now. He has a mirror so he can look out of the window without being seen to be looking.'

'Then you shouldn't be talking to me,' he said. 'Guilt by association.'

'He'll tell my mum,' she said. 'His sister. This is her stall. She'll tell him to mind his own business. Then they'll have a shouting match. Brother and sister at it as if they were teenagers.' She laughed again. 'It's so silly. Big frogs, little ponds. Or should it be little frogs, little ponds?' She shrugged. 'Just make sure you keep in with me and David, and you'll be OK.'

'Who's David?'

'Uncle David runs the crematorium. And doesn't get on with Saul, not one bit.' She paused for a second, then added, 'Saul is the older brother, by a year or so.'

'Saul's enemy is David's friend? Very biblical.' He was trying to recollect his Sunday school days. David and Saul. A couple of Hebrew Kings. David slew Goliath. What had Saul done? Oh yes, got rid of someone's husband by putting him in the front line of a battle. Or was that David? He was trying not to stare at the gap in her teeth, but it was difficult not to, and so he had to look away as he sieved the remnants of his Old Testament knowledge.

'Granddad was quite a puritan,' she said. 'He's long dead and both his sons are on the board, and have a cemetery to run. There are some long, fractious meetings, so my mum says. She's on the board too.'

'I can see myself being a good pal of David,' he said. He recalled what he'd come for. 'Can I leave these tools here for a minute? I've got to go back to my van for my thermos and sandwiches.'

'Of course you can. I've some tea brewing myself,' she said. 'You can have a cuppa here.'

'That'll be nice,' he said. 'But I'll need my own, for later. Where can I leave the tools?'

'Put them by the shed.' She indicated the wooden building behind her. 'They'll be safe. I'll have your tea poured out by the time you're back.'

'I hope I'm not getting you in trouble with Mr Coe, Saul I mean.'

'We don't get on anyway,' she said. 'Not now, not since...' She stopped and reflected, and then continued. 'When I first started here, a couple of months back, he used to come out and talk to me all the time. Then he tried it on, uncle or not, can you believe that? I had to remind him he was married to my aunt.' She pursed her lips. 'He didn't like that.'

'I'm sure he didn't,' said Jack, intrigued by the personal history.

'What was I supposed to do?' she exclaimed, opening her hands to show lack of choice. 'Tell him I didn't fancy him?

That he was way too old? Threaten to tell my mum, his sister?'

'Doesn't matter how you said it,' said Jack. 'You hurt his feelings. You made him feel guilty.'

She grimaced. 'I didn't want him all over me. Who does he think he is?'

'Fair enough,' said Jack as he placed the various tools by the wall of the hut. 'Back in a mo'.'

'I'll have the tea ready.'

Jack walked back to his vehicle. Saul made enemies all around. You have to get on with people. A big lesson he'd learnt from Alcohol Halt. Far better than getting drunk and raging at them.

His mood had lightened. Certainly one way of getting Maria out of his system was to try elsewhere. He was already running ahead of himself. He didn't even know the flower woman's name. She could already be fixed up. Just have a cup of tea with her. Don't make plans, even if his hormones were well ahead of such advice.

Chapter 4

Jack stretched his arm into the van, and from the passenger seat he brought out his thermos and sandwiches. They were in a blue-grey fabric bag with a shoulder strap that he'd bought for a pound a couple of years back, though the stitching was now going on the side of the bag. Buy a new one or sew this one? It'd be a waste to throw it away.

He locked the van and looked up at the sky. All the blue had gone. A layer of whitish grey was overhead but ominously darker in the west. He'd get his cup of tea, then set to work. The footings had to be put in while the weather held. Was the florist spoken for? He'd have to put a casual question to her, as if he didn't care.

His phone rang. Jack pulled it from his overall pocket. Alison, his ex. What did she want so early? Probably him to look after Mia this evening. That was usually it. A date, she was always going out with someone.

'Hello, Alison,' he said warily. 'What can I do for you?'

'Where are you?' she said.

'Outside Forest Gate cemetery. Why?'

'Just up the road. Good,' she exclaimed. 'Water is coming through the bathroom ceiling and down into the kitchen. It's going to ruin everything.'

'Turn the stopcock off,' he said.

'I don't know where it is.'

'You've been in the house over six months and you don't know where the stopcock is?' He laughed. He shouldn't, but it came in spite of more measured thought.

She cut him short. 'Can you fix it, Jack? Please. I've got a staff meeting. I must get off. Do me a favour, and I'll owe you one.'

He perked up. A chance to get a brownie point instead of a ticking off.

'I'll be right over.'

'Thanks, Jack. I'll leave the key under the bin. Please come right away.'

She closed the call. Jack rested against the van, scratching his cheek. The florist had invited him for tea. He didn't want to blow that one. But Alison had a leak which could only get worse and soak through the ceiling plaster. He could be there in a few minutes, turn off the stopcock to stop water coming into the house. That should halt the leak. Then with luck get back to the florist for a lukewarm cup of tea. Later on, go back to Alison, after he'd got the footings in, to fix whatever the problem was.

So organised. Sex and work fixed. Jack got in the van and headed off. Pity he didn't have the florist's number. But they'd just met, hadn't got to that point. If they ever would. He suddenly recalled, he'd hardly thought of Maria in the last hour. The therapy of busyness. It was hard being told that it wouldn't work out, that you weren't right – especially when you thought you were. The text had been a wet towel flicked in his face. She'd met someone else. Hopefully, he had too.

Alison lived straight up the road, about quarter of a mile away. But he'd hit the school run. His ex lived opposite Woodgrange Infants school and the world seemed to be heading that way. There was a stream of slow traffic up the road in both directions, stopping and starting as parents dropped children off. Why couldn't the kids walk? Because of the traffic. Obvious. They might get run over. So they sat in cars, eating sweets and getting fat. Collectively it could be sorted out. One solution was on the pavement alongside; a string of small children in yellow high-viz jackets walking in pairs, holding hands. There was an adult at the front and one at the back, the one at the rear held a pole with a circular sign saying 'Walking Bus'. They were keeping up with Jack.

This was useless. He was barely moving and the closer that he got to the school, the harder it would be to park. He spotted a parking spot and pulled in. And then was out the van and striding up the road, past the walking bus, all but running. He just hoped he didn't need tools or he'd have to go back to the van.

Outside the school, traffic had stalled in both directions. A mother had stopped her car in the middle of the road, and oblivious to the hooting behind her was taking her little boy to the school gate. Jack watched as he strode on, pleased to be out of the melee and on foot. The mother kissed the boy, ushered him into the playground and ran back to her car, all but getting run over as she crossed the road. She was apologising to the driver behind, other cars hooting, as Jack scurried up Alison's short path. Under the bin, he found the house key. So far so good.

Jack opened the front door. He listened, couldn't hear anything at first because of the traffic noise. Ah yes, running water. He stayed by the front door, knowing this was where the stopcock usually is, where the mains water comes into the house. Often a little cupboard or some pull-up in the floorboards. There was nothing in the walls. He couldn't see anything on the floor. Jack lifted the floor mat. There it was, a small door cut in the floorboards with a ring to lift it up. Except it wouldn't lift. It was jammed with grit. He pulled at the ring for maybe half a minute then gave up and ran into the kitchen. Water was dripping down from the centre of the ceiling; some of it down the light and its shade.

Jack opened the cutlery drawer. He needed a lever. There were forks, knives and spoons in the drawer. He needed something substantial. There was a meat skewer or whatever you call it, the steel thing you stuffed in the joint to hold it while you sliced it. He took the skewer and a long sharp knife and ran back to the hallway with them. He put the skewer in the ring and tried to lever the ring up. The small trapdoor resisted. Jack scraped some of the muck round the sides of the little door with the knife. He tried again with the skewer – and the door lifted. In the space, under the floor-boards, was the pipe coming in from the roadway and into the house, with its stopcock. He attempted to turn it off. Jammed. This was where his hammer would be useful. He gave the stopcock a clump with the skewer. And again. That did it. And Jack was able to turn off the incoming water. Then went into the kitchen to check.

Water was still dripping down from the ceiling. Well, it would for a while. He took the basin out of the sink and put it under the main drips. Then turned on the cold water tap over the sink. It hissed and spluttered, water came out for a few seconds and then the flow stopped. Good. No more water was coming into the house. He thought for a second. The leak though could be from the hot water tank in the loft. It might be overfull and so might continue to leak if the overflow was blocked. He turned on the hot water tap and let it run for a minute or so. That would take a few inches off the level of the hot water tank, and no more would be flowing in as he'd turned off the incoming water.

Jack left the kitchen and climbed the stairs. He went into the upstairs bathroom. Water was dripping off the light fitting, slowing even as he watched. But water and electricity wasn't a good combination.

He left the bathroom, and there, on the landing, was what he was looking for, the fuse box. He put the light on in the hallway, then opened the fuse box. He flipped the fuse switches until the hall light went off. It would be on a ring circuit with the other lights upstairs, including the one in the bathroom with the dripping water. The other fuses he left on. It wouldn't do to turn the fridge and freezer off, and be responsible for decomposing food. Alison would never let him forget that.

That was the emergency work done, though he'd better get back here before Alison got home in the evening, and sort out the problem. She was well practised at hectoring, being a head teacher. Errant schoolchildren or ex-husbands posed no problems.

Anyway, leak stopped and safe. He must get back to work.

He left, locking the front door. He kept the key as he'd be coming back once he had the footings down. And strode quickly down the road to his van. The school run had thinned out. Ten, fifteen minutes, that's all it had lasted. Children were lined up in the school playground. He recalled taking Mia to school, the same regime. She was at secondary school now, so no lining up, but there were other indignities she filled him in on.

Jack glanced at the sky, then at his watch. 9 am and he hadn't done any paid work yet. He might get something off Alison when he'd fixed the leak, might not. From time to time she'd given him the odd twenty when he was looking after their daughter and he was short. So she might consider this job payback.

Time to get earning.

Chapter 5

The builder and Kim were talking and Saul had no wish to confront them. He'd been watching them through the mirror. She was laughing at something. Probably talking about him. Didn't they have any work to do? What on earth did they have to say to each other? And there, the builder was heading for the gate, he'd left a bucket and some tools by her shed wall. What did that signify? That he was coming back. It was obvious what was going to happen. The builder shouldn't be here at all by rights. Totally against policy. His brother had broken the rule, and the rest of the board had gone along with him. Ridiculous. How can you run a concern like that?

Maureen glanced at him from time to time, noting him looking into the mirror to see out of the window. He caught her looking, was about to tell her off for not working but instead picked up a clipboard and told her he would be doing a site inspection. If anything urgent came in, phone him. In the meantime, continue with the meeting papers. And he left the office by the back door. He came out into a narrow alleyway, bordered by the cemetery wall and the office. A little further, beyond the office, was the workers' mess hut, a long wooden shed, utterly practical, that might serve as well for battery hens, especially when shuttered.

He was agitated, could barely concentrate on anything. It was the meeting this afternoon. They were out to get him, that was clear. He'd seen Nora and David conspiring in corners. Well, he wasn't going to have it. He'd done a good job here up till now. Why change things? Except nothing was so logical. It was all personalities. Bert Greene, the solicitor, would support him. Could he get Kim onside? She was being voted on to the board today. He'd been stupid, making a play, so silly, so near home. It wasn't that he didn't love Sarah, his wife, but sex was impossible there. And there was Kim, just out the office window, in touching distance, and almost divorced. So thoughtless. He should apologise.

Later.

Saul pushed the door of the workers' mess hut. It was open; it shouldn't have been. He went in.

The mess room was strictly functional. A long wooden table with benches on either side, a couple of spare chairs. There was a row of eight dark green lockers along the rear wall. A side wall had the sink with the china cupboard above. And there was Tony Evans in his baggy overalls at the sink, drinking water from a glass. Saul had never liked Tony. He could sniff the insolence, coming off him like aftershave.

Seeing Coe, Tony poured the remaining water into the sink and put the glass in the basin. He wiped his mouth with his sleeve.

'Just getting a drink,' he said with the hint of a grin.

Saul blasted at him. 'At this time of the morning! You have come all the way back here just to get a drink? There are a dozen taps on site.' He swung his arm as if to point them all out. 'You can't come in here every five minutes to get a drink. Suppose everyone did it? How's any work going to get done?'

'I came for the loppers actually.' Tony indicated them, lying on a bench by the long wooden table.

'Why didn't you take them with you in the first place?'

'I didn't realise how overgrown the tree was. Could poke someone's eye out.'

'Couldn't it have waited till tea break? You could've got them then.' Saul paced the floorboards, taking a semicircle round Tony, his eye on him all the time as if he might escape. 'But no, better to waste ten minutes going back and forth and getting paid for it.'

Evans was shuffling on the spot, biting his lip, knowing it wouldn't help to better his boss. 'I'll get back to work.'

Saul was rocking backwards and forwards breathing heavily. 'Next time, take what you need when you go out. If you forget anything, pick it up during your break. Do you get me? Or do I need to write it down for you?'

'I understand, Mr Coe.'

'What's Phil doing this morning, and Tamaz?'

'Tamaz is out with the digger, digging the graves for this afternoon. Phil is going round the roads with the leafer...'

'If you see 'em, tell I'll be along shortly. Now hop to it.' He pointed to the door and through it, across the cemetery to where Tony had left the mower. 'I don't want to catch you skiving again.'

Tony hesitated as if to say something, thought better of it, picked up the loppers and went out the door.

For a few seconds, Saul stood frozen. He'd been in manager mode while dressing down Tony. Now alone, he was the Chairman under attack. Why was life so difficult? The meeting. He needed allies. He had standards. That's what he was fighting, sloppiness. The chopping and changing that was his brother's way of working. The builder and Kim chatting as if they had nothing else to do. This was not a social club.

It was stupid to blow up at Tony. The man wasn't worth it. And he must not have a go at Kim, rather the reverse. He could do things for her. Make her realise that. Not sex, forget that aberration. He must encourage the next generation.

He left the mess hut, locking up after him. Then into the yard, where the builder wanted to leave his vehicle. Saul's car was there and a few belonging to the workers, out of the way, so the tractor, digger and runabouts could come and go. It was fenced off from the cemetery with high iron railings.

Saul went into the cemetery itself, through the gate, locking it after him. All those conkers. They'd have to be cleared away. He was raving at little things, as if even nature was in conspiracy against him. He must get himself together. Stay in control.

From here, he could see the flower stall. Kim was watering pots. The builder wasn't there. No doubt he'd be back. Sex on his mind when he should be at work. Coe headed for her stall, kicking conkers and leaves out of the way. He should go to church, pray. God knew his wickedness.

Coe slowed as he neared Kim. He straightened his jacket, then his tie. His shoes were neat.

'Might I have a word, Kim?'

She turned as he walked towards her. She put down the watering can.

'Of course,' she said, with a half smile, managing to hold her hand away from her mouth.

He began awkwardly, not knowing how to broach it. 'I should have spoken to you before, but these things are difficult. Especially in families.' He stopped, no point rambling. 'I want to apologise. There was no call for my behaviour. It was a foolish whim. You were quite right to chastise me.'

'You have Aunty Sarah to think about,' she said.

'I do. It was awful. Sarah needs me. Please accept my apology. It will never happen again.'

'I accept your apology,' she said. 'I know you have problems, but you also have responsibilities.'

'I do. And thank you for being so understanding. Life isn't easy with Sarah. But no excuses.' He stopped, closed his eyes. 'I am grateful, Kim. Please don't tell your mother.'

'I haven't,' she said, 'and I won't. Providing you don't bother me again.'

'Don't worry, don't worry,' he said, pushing his hands to ward off doubt. 'I'm pleased you are joining the board.'

'Thank you.'

'You are a mature young woman. And the new generation has to be ready to take over in their turn. This is a family concern.'

She had begun watering plants again, almost he felt in dismissal.

'I think there's likely to be a vote of confidence in my role as chairman of the board,' he went on. 'Will you vote for me, Kim?'

She didn't reply for a few seconds, watering the pots.

'I don't know, I'm not sure,' she mumbled.

'I was thinking of giving you a present,' he said.

Kim stopped watering, and turned to him. 'A present? What?'

'I was thinking of five thousand pounds. To make up for past neglect. To show goodwill.'

'Ten.'

'What?'

'Ten thousand pounds and you have my vote.'

He took a step back. 'That's a lot of money, Kim.'

'If I vote for you, I'll have a fight on with my mother and Uncle David... There'll be blood on the carpet.'

He considered her counter offer, turning his back and strolling aimlessly, scratching his head. It would be a terrible meeting. That was certain. But ten thousand pounds for a single vote? Then again, once paid, she would have forgiven him.

A sin erased on his card.

Chapter 6

In the florist's hut was a small Calor gas ring. It was only ever used for making tea. The kettle was whistling away when Kim went in. She hadn't had any customers yet. Not surprising as it wasn't half nine yet, early for a graveside visit. She turned off the gas and with an oven glove, lifted the kettle and poured the hot water into the teapot.

Just as well the public couldn't see in here. There were only three mugs, and they could all do with a scrub out. Months of quick rinsing had hardened the brown stains round the insides. One day, she'd take them home, scrub them out. But did it matter? Tea stains did you no harm. Every teapot was coated with them. Layer upon layer like tree rings. So much to worry about if you let yourself go down that road.

Housework was for housewives. She would get by, but not make it her religion. Too much cleanliness wasn't healthy. It pursued you to the grave. Her house with Brad had been too clean; she'd never liked it. Brad was hot on dust. He'd wanted their sitting room to be as sterile as a hotel suite. All that polishing and vacuuming, not that she did it, but was surrounded by the noise and hustle to keep whites whiter, to outlaw the last speck of dirt. What was the point? Dust to dust.

What had happened to the builder? He'd said he'd be a few minutes. That had been twenty minutes ago. Time enough for her to make ten thousand pounds. All she had to do was vote for Uncle Saul. Her mother would go crazy. She might guess what had gone on. Well, so what? Kim wasn't staying at home much longer.

There was a small mirror on the wall; she glanced into it, showed her teeth and grimaced. You can't stay in the house because you have a tooth missing. It had to come out, it had become so loose. The dentist said the gums must harden before he could put in a crown. She fingered the gap. It was evidence of mortality, slow erosion. The gap was in the centre. The focus. Really, so silly to be so obsessed. She'd only been speaking to a builder. But we judge so quickly, size up faces and bodies, the colour of skin, a solitary pimple. Did the gap make her ugly? Well, she wasn't modelling. And models pouted without opening their mouths. Who would know how bad their teeth were?

To put it plainly, she fancied the builder and wanted him to fancy her. He'd be along sooner or later; he'd left his tools here. And tomorrow was her dental appointment. She would be transformed. Of course, she wouldn't. Did it affect her figure? No. But yes, it all added up, you take someone as a whole. A pretty face enhances a figure, an ugly one negates it. She could see he'd been looking at the gap, even embarrassed by it. So daft, so juvenile. There were women with burnt faces, with blotches all over them. She was like a teenager obsessing over a spot. Heavens – it would be gone tomorrow. But then would her chance with him be gone too?

She'd spoken to the builder for a few minutes. And look what she was doing. Yes, he was good looking. But what was he really like? How can you tell, until he swings a punch. Relationships are impossible to judge at the outset, trying to get the whole of someone out of a smile and banter. Besides, he'd see her tomorrow with perfect teeth. A very fine swan indeed.

Except he hadn't come back. His tools were still there. He'd only gone to his van to pick up his sandwiches. And then Uncle Saul had come with his offer. She couldn't really believe that she was ten thousand pounds richer. All she had to do was raise her hand at the meeting.

Not quite all.

She'd have her tea, and if the builder came, he came. And if he didn't, he didn't. What a daft thing to say. What happened happened. Of course. But that didn't make it any better or worse. She didn't believe in fate anyway. You created your life, you didn't wait for a fairy godmother. Or she'd still be with Brad, weeping and waiting by the fireside.

Kim poured milk into a cup, hesitated and poured some into another. She looked again in the mirror. It was no different, the same humdrum face, the same chasm. You can't see it when you kiss. But you could poke your tongue into it, if you so desired.

Stop this, stop this instant. Smash all the mirrors in the kingdom. No one was perfect. We sex ourselves up with make-up and clothes, exaggerate, lie. It was dumb, it was vain. There were too many people in the world, sizing up each other, making snap judgements on voice and accent, hair, weight, colour, clothing, shoes, make-up, no make-up, nails to kill with, height. Instantly ticking boxes, computing the overall score. She was down the table today. No, she was ten thousand pounds up. She was climbing rapidly. Tomorrow, with perfect teeth, she'd be the league leader.

Plans. She must work on her plans. She wasn't going to stay at her mother's a day longer than she had to. She had the money, she had to get moving.

'Hello!' A woman's voice from outside.

Kim came out of the hut with a smile, managing to hold down her hand. She couldn't keep apologising. But it was only the old lady with her basket on wheels. A regular. She was holding up a small pot of primroses, with its scattering of yellow and red flowers. Kim liked old people. They didn't size you up and down. The old lady didn't care a hoot about the gap in her teeth. She was wiry, all wrinkles and grey hair, smiling back.

'Would you like a cup of tea?' said Kim.

Chapter 7

'Sorry,' Jack said. 'I got an emergency phone call from my ex. She had a leak coming through the ceiling, and could I sort it out pronto? She's only up the road.' He pointed in that direction. 'I owe her a favour or two, that's why I'm late for tea. Any left?'

'It's somewhat stewed,' said Kim, brushing the blonde hair off her brow, leaving a smudge where she'd been handling plants. 'Stay there.'

She went into the hut. Jack had come back in a rush, relieved she wasn't offended. Should he ask her out? It would be a good idea, stop him thinking about Maria. She could only say no. *I'm engaged, getting married this weekend. Sorry.*

Dopy. He must get the footings done here, then get back to Alison's later. Ask the flower girl out. Go on. Quick cuppa. See how it goes. Must get to work.

Kim came out with his tea. 'Almost a cup,' she said, indicating two thirds of a cup. 'Still warm.' She handed it over. 'You don't have to drink it if it's too stewed.'

Jack took a sip. 'Drinkable,' he said. 'Some of the stuff I've been offered...' He winced at the memory. 'One site where I was working, the boss bought the cheapest teabags going. More like old rope than tea.'

'I was wondering what happened to you,' she said. 'You wouldn't just abandon your tools.'

'I'm a slave to the phone,' he said with a shrug. The gap in her teeth gave her a piratical look. Work on that. Up the rigging. Together in the crow's nest.

'You said your ex called,' she said.

'Yes. I was about to come back here,' he said, 'and I got the call about the leak...'

'You still get on with her?'

He shrugged. 'I wouldn't call us friends. We have a daughter, Mia, so I try to get on with Alison. But she can be difficult.'

'How's that?'

'Oh, she's a head teacher. Bossy.' He didn't want to go into his past, his drunken days, when he'd been less than a model husband. 'And yourself?' he asked, wanting to get away from his own history.

She smiled, her hand half going to her mouth, then realising it wasn't needed. 'I'm almost divorced,' she said. 'Two weeks to go.' She indicated her gap. 'He did that. Brad. And a few other things. Now he's in jail. Good, so good.' She paused then added ruefully, 'Not for hitting me. I'm a minor crime compared to armed robbery. A four million pound bank job in Birmingham.'

'That the one where the security guard was killed?'

'The very one. And that's why he's doing twenty years.'

Complications, but she was free. Jack was intrigued, but would have to get the rest of the tale later. He had to go, he wanted to stay. He didn't know what to say. So he drank the tea, the empty cup awkward in his hand, lacking the will to put it down. She took it, fingers lingering. Their eyes held, a finger curled round his.

'Would you like to come out with me?' he said.

'I was wondering if you were going to ask.'

'Tonight?'

She sucked her lip hesitantly. 'I've got to see a house tonight. How about you come along? It'd be useful to have a builder's eye.'

'Is this work or what?'

'We'll only be there fifteen minutes. Then I'll take you out to dinner. Fair swap?'

'Just looking over a house?'
'You won't need your drill.'

Chapter 8

At last he was working, earning his keep. A lot had intervened. Saul Coe with his nonsense, then Alison's plea for him to come round, and then the liaison at the flower stall. He'd hardly thought of Maria at all, that curt rejection had receded like a train going backwards into a tunnel. Last night, it had been all enveloping; this morning, he had a job to do, an ill tempered manager to work round and a date this evening. Maria was a dot on the horizon.

He wondered at his feelings for Maria. How he could forget her so easily now, when last night he couldn't sleep at her rejection. Not Maria herself then, but the brusque parting. Why couldn't she have told him face to face? It didn't matter anyway. She'd probably met someone else, that was the truth of it. Maybe she'd been seeing whoever while she was going out with Jack. She had been less available the last week or two. And now she'd made her decision. The mating game is full of deceit. Kissing one and thinking of another.

He'd been there.

The breeze had picked up, catching in the high trees in the wooded areas ahead of him. When working outside, Jack was a regular sky watcher, so dependent on the weather. He was suddenly reminded that he'd left the plastic sheeting in the van. Something forgotten. If the rain came down he'd need to cover the concrete. A real downpour would hold back the setting. And it had to be firm tomorrow for Jack to begin bricklaying.

He'd removed the grass. It was short, and not difficult to get under and lever out with a spade. He now had a heap of turf and wondered what he should do with it. There must be a dump in the cemetery yard, but with Coe's policy of non-cooperation, he couldn't use it. If it came to the worst he'd have to take it to the van and cart it away. In fact, Alison had a compost heap in her back yard, and he had to go back there, so that was an option.

With the grass cover gone, Jack marked out the extent of the footings with pegs and line. A long side of two and half metres with two short sides at either end. Into the space would go a bench. On the footings, he'd build a low brick wall. Mrs Little was having the bench made; she would attach a memorial plaque to her husband. To complete the bower, the wall would have a number of wooden uprights attached to the outside. Onto these, he would attach wooden trellis, with a trellis roof. And that would be his work completed. Mrs Little then took over. She was going to plant climbing roses in three large urns, yellow, red and white. In a few years they would trail over the trellis, grow over the roof and drip down at the back and front. He could imagine it being a pleasant place to sit on a summer's day, with roses all around. Quite why this had so upset Coe, he couldn't fathom. Politics, the woman in the office had said. Maureen, that was her name.

Politics left Jack no wiser. Meanness, maybe. Someone who pulls legs off spiders for kicks.

The trench for the wall footings had to be a little wider than twice the width of a brick, about ten inches, as the wall would be a double brick thickness. About 6 inches deep. Into the trench would go 4 inches of concrete. The first course of bricks would bond to the footings and be half in the trench and half out. The little space left in the trench would be filled in with soil, so just the wall was visible on its solid foundation.

Digging the trench was annoying, the spade striking pieces of gravestone and funeral decorations which Jack threw in a heap. A piece of an angel's wing, the broken rim of an urn, a small ear – maybe from a cherub, and miscellaneous stone pieces that he couldn't identify. The area must have been cleared recently. Presumably the bodies had been left in the ground. Or had the remnants been gathered up? And then what? Buried collectively in a pit, or burnt. What else would they do, these practical cemetery people?

There was only so much space and everyone dies. Give it fifty years, till there's no one around who remembers you, then clear the ground for the next lot. All very businesslike, quite sensible use of limited space, but Jack felt discomfort at these careless bits and pieces he was digging up. Forget all that 'never forgotten' and 'always in our hearts' engraved on the tombstones, and read 'fifty years if you're lucky'.

His spade struck more debris. More funeral decoration, he reckoned, as he picked up the soil encrusted piece. But this was a bone. He cleared off the soil with his fingers. It was a lower jaw with half its teeth in place. Human, but male, female – he had no idea. The bone was cracked and crazed. What should he do with it? Stupid to take it to the office. He couldn't imagine much sentimentality there. The cemetery workers must find this stuff every day. He twisted the jaw in his hands. What was life like for you? Were you a total pig or a pussycat? Did you suffer much when you were dying?

He threw the bone on the heap of debris. As he worked on, the jaw kept catching his eye, appealing. What did it expect of him? Like a ghost watching him. At last, he'd had enough of it. He took the jaw to a nearby copse of trees and buried it a foot down, stamping hard on the soil covering it. Perhaps it would be found again and perhaps it wouldn't. Rest in peace, whoever you were.

By the time Jack stopped for his tea break he'd laid half the footings. He'd been working quickly, adding water to the concrete mix, turning it until it was homogeneous and then shovelling the concrete in the shallow trench. As he drank from his thermos, sitting on his upturned wheelbarrow, he felt spots of rain. The clouds were considerably darker. He must finish laying the concrete before that lot came down.

Jack cut short his tea break. There were two bags and a half of concrete left, about right for the rest of the footings. He poured half on to his mixing board, made a crater in the middle of the heap and poured in water from his bucket.

And then he was stumbling, catching the shovel under his feet, scrambling to stay upright, dropping the bucket. As he fell to the ground, his hand slapped onto the shovel blade.

He sat upright. That was daft, leaving the shovel under his feet. And then he noted blood seeping through the mud on the back of his hand. He'd need to get that patched up. Though he wouldn't be asking Mr Coe for his first aid box. But he had to get finished here first.

The rain was coming down steadily. Jack got down to work, trying to ignore the rain and blood on his hand. He shovelled the concrete into the trench of the footings. The downpour increased as he made up the last of the concrete. He was wet through. Too bad, it was only water. He shovelled as rapidly as he could, as if he were a machine. Load the shovel, stride to the trench, let it go, back to the heap, shovel up. Repeat. The repetition built up heat, almost enjoyable, in spite of the teeming rain.

When all the concrete was laid in the trench, he levelled it with the float, pressing out the lumpy bits. Now he must get it covered. Temporarily, he used the empty sacks, using debris to stop them blowing off in the wind. But there weren't enough sacks, too many gaps.

He raced off into the rain toward his van, cursing Saul Coe. If he'd allowed Jack to park here, it would have taken a minute to get the sheeting, but no – he had to go back to the gates. Up the roadway, past the crematorium where a new group of mourners had come with their cars, umbrellas up, rushing into the hall. Breathless, he passed the flower stall. Kim wasn't there, presumably sheltering in the hut. And on past the office where Coe might or might not have been watching for him. Jack took care not to look, to not know of Coe's pleasure in his soaking.

He reached his van outside the gate. Once there, he collapsed in the passenger seat, catching his breath. Blood had set on the back of his hand, like a ruby with strands holding it in place. Jack leaned over the seat and pulled out a large plastic sheet. And he was out again in the rain, running through the cemetery gates, splashing through the puddles, with the sheet over his head, making little difference in the driving rain, the droplets splattering on the tarmac. Lightning flashed, a bright fork dashing to earth beyond the trees, followed almost instantly by thunder, rumbling, and re-rumbling. The storm was almost overhead. Soon it would pass. If he wasn't sharp, he joked with himself, the rain would stop before he could cover the footings.

Puffed out, he continued at a walk. The cemetery was empty, the treetops thrashing. He was so utterly wet more rain hardly mattered, but the concrete had to be kept free of water if he was to lay the bricks tomorrow.

At the site, Jack unfolded the sheet and spread it over the footings. The sheet was ample to cover it all. Round the edges Jack placed funeral debris to hold the sheet down. Done. He shook his wet hair like a dog coming out of a pond, and wiped it back. Time to get his hand seen to. Choices. Forget Mr Coe. Kim was unlikely. What about the crematorium? On the grounds that my enemy's enemy is my friend.

He threw his tools into the wheelbarrow and headed with it to the crematorium, the rain having its last vengeful go at him. He glanced down at the injured hand on the wheelbarrow handle and saw the rain was cleansing the wound.

Virtue is its own reward.

At the crematorium, he left the wheelbarrow against the wall near the double doors. Too bad if Mr Coe saw it. The likelihood wasn't great in this downpour. And he went in, wiping his boots thoroughly on the mat. The heat in the foyer was welcome. To his right, there was another set of double doors. Over the doors, an electronic sign saying: *Quiet Please. Service in Progress.*

A little way beyond were stairs going down into the basement. Where no doubt the cremations took place. Across from the hall was a door labelled David Coe, Manager. Jack knocked on the door.

A middle aged man in a smart grey suit opened up. He was on the portly side, his hair grey and full, receding at the front.

'Hello,' he said. He snapped his fingers. 'I know who you are. Kim told me. You're the builder working on Ruth's memorial plot.'

'I am. And I've cut my hand.' Jack showed the back of his hand. 'I wondered if you had a first aid box.'

'Yes, we have one,' said David.

'I couldn't ask your brother; he and I got off on the wrong foot.'

David chuckled. 'Kim told me. Not the friendliest knife in the box is our Saul. Let's get you cleaned up.'

He came out of the office and locked the door behind him. 'There's a staff washroom downstairs. Jack of All Trades, is it?'

'It is.' He must've seen the van.

'I'm David Coe. We'll shake hands when you've cleaned up.'

He led Jack down the stone steps, into a long, austere hallway. No decoration here. No windows, plain brick. To one side, three coffins were on trolleys. A man in a heavy, silvered apron was unscrewing fittings on one of the coffins with an electric screwdriver. He gave David a half wave and continued working. From the rear came a constant roar, where there were three metal doors at trolley height.

David took him into a side washroom. The floor was tiled in white, as were the walls to halfway up. There were two sinks, a cupboard, toilet stalls and a shower unit. David opened the cupboard and handed Jack a towel.

'Wipe yourself down. I won't be a sec.'

He left Jack wiping his hair, face and arms. And then carefully around the wound; he couldn't evade getting mud on the towel. The blood had clotted. He took off his shirt and twisted it over the sink, squeezing water out. His vest would have to dry against his body, but with the heat down here it wouldn't take long. He put the shirt back on and washed his hands at the sink with the liquid soap, carefully dabbing at the wound. And then dried himself thoroughly, finishing just as David returned with two plastic chairs and a first aid box. He sat Jack in a chair and sat on the other himself. He opened the box which had various sizes of sticking plasters, bandages, cotton wool, scissors and anti-septic cream.

'Rub a bit of this in.' He handed over the cream. 'And wipe it off with the cotton wool.' He sorted out plasters of the right size.

When the first aid was completed, they went back out to the main basement area where the worker was pushing a coffin on a trolley to the ovens. He had put on a helmet which had a frontage of darkened glass.

'All the latest equipment,' said David, seeing Jack watching.

The man halted the trolley near one of the ovens. He pressed a button on a remote control, and a platform came out from under the oven. The worker pushed the trolley to meet the end, and then slid the coffin on to the platform. He pressed another button, the platform slid into its recess carrying the coffin with it, as, at the same time, the oven door lifted like a shutter. The coffin was swept into the oven so quickly, the door then closing it off. Jack wanted a replay to check how it had happened. He'd had just time to see a column of blinding flame as the door came down, hiding the contents.

'That's hot,' he exclaimed as a blast of heat reached him. 'What fuel do you use?'

'Gas. The temperature is around 900 degrees Celsius. In 90 minutes or so all the flesh, guts and clothing are burnt away. We make sure shoes, jewellery, or any metal adornment are removed first.'

'It seems a waste to burn a coffin.'

David shrugged. 'No more than putting a coffin in the earth. We simply destroy it quicker than the worms. Though in the US they use cardboard coffins.'

'Good idea. No point wasting good wood. What happens after the body's been burnt?'

'We leave it to cool, then scrape the ash into a gutter. At that stage, the ash is lumpy with bone fragments. We take a sample, sift out any metal bits, and put the sample in a mill to crush it to a uniform powder. That's put into an urn to be collected by relatives. If they want it. Some don't.' He shrugged. 'I can understand that. There's nothing human left behind. It's just a grey powder.'

Jack was struck by how industrial it was. The everyday roasting of human corpses. It was a job of work, as it had to be, a process.

'How many do you do in a day?'

'About ten.'

A light was flashing on the side wall by a waist high door. The worker came over, taking off his helmet as he did so. He pressed a button and the door slid into a recess, revealing a coffin. He drew it out onto a trolley. Lying by it was a clipboard which the man ticked.

'I thought coffins slid down from the hall straight into the oven,' said Jack. 'Dumb really, when you think about it.'

'There's no mystery,' said David. 'The bodies come down in the lift and we put them in the oven when one of them is ready. When we're busy we have a line of trolleys with coffins waiting their turn. I give a hand, from time to time, when I'm free from meeting and greeting. We try to do the day's business the same day. Can't always, if we're extra busy. Might be a couple of coffins waiting first thing in the morning. We get them done before the next arrivals.'

'Do you ever give out the wrong ashes?'

David laughed and shook a finger at Jack. 'Firstly, would I admit that? Secondly, no. We label everything, do the paperwork as each coffin comes down, then as it goes into the oven and when the ashes are milled. You have to be methodical.'

Jack watched the worker unscrewing the fittings on the coffin that had just come down.

'What do you do with the handles and fittings?' he said.

'What would you do with them?' asked David.

'Sell them back to the coffin maker.'

David smiled. 'No comment. Though a lot are plastic these days; they flash off in the flame. Let's go up and have a cup of tea.'

They went up the stairs, into the decorated area and natural light, like a modern church in contrast with the factory business of the basement. David led him into his office. It was small, neat, with just room enough for a desk, two guest chairs, a cupboard with tea things on top, and some shelving.

'There's no windows downstairs,' said Jack, looking out at the rain and mourners scurrying to their cars, umbrellas up, jackets pulled over heads.

David turned on the kettle. 'Most people don't want to know what happens down there,' he said. 'Some would be

disturbed, though it's hard to think why. This is a crematorium. Our job is to burn bodies.'

'Too much like a factory for comfort,' said Jack.

David shrugged. 'Yes, it is industrial. But think about it.
There are over seven and a half billion people on the planet.
If they were all buried, there'd be graveyards the size of
towns, growing every year. It's poor use of land.'

'I can see that,' mused Jack. 'I'll consider my options over
the next forty years, all being well.'

'I'll be cremated,' said David flatly. 'I've written that in
my will.'

'What about these forest burials people go for these
days?'

'It feeds the trees, I suppose,' said David, 'but if you really
want to fertilise the land then you should be composted. For
crops, I mean. There's a lot of useful nitrogen and trace
elements in a human corpse. You would put a heap of
bodies in a silo, with worms... The methane given off could
fuel the machinery, any extra fed into the grid, and the
compost created goes on to the fields to fertilise crops. Efficient usage. Why waste all that nitrogen? Not that I can see it
happening. We're too finicky. Heads full of fairy tales and
bible stories. My brother's going to be buried. Very tradi-
tional, that's Saul all over. He didn't tell me himself. We
don't talk much. Nora, our sister, Kim's mother, tells me he
has a tombstone in his garage, all ready and waiting.' He
laughed. 'I can't understand him some days. He blows up
over nothing. Like the memorial bower you are building.
His personality changed after the accident.'

'What accident?'

David poured the hot water into the tea pot, adding the
tea bags and stirring.

'Saul was in a car crash. He was hit head-on by a drunken
driver who was killed. Seven years ago now. Saul was in a
coma for two weeks. Sarah, his wife, that's the saddest tale.

She's in a wheelchair, paralysed from the waist down, has several fulltime carers. She can't speak, communicates through a laptop computer. It's hard work having a conversation with her, but you have to try.' He threw up his hands. 'What can you do! She was a beautiful woman. A solicitor. Her partners made sure she got the best of settlements, but really, when I think what she was...' He stopped. 'I think it might have been better if she'd died.' He held up a hand. 'Sorry. I shouldn't have said that. Don't repeat it, please.'

'Of course not.' David handed Jack a cup of tea. 'Thank you for the first aid and tea. It's good to be dry.' He stopped, adding what had been bothering him at the crematorium. 'Does it affect you, dealing with the dead all day?'

'You get used to it in no time. Ask my wife, ask my kids, if they think I'm odd. The dead are dead as far as I'm concerned. No more alive than meat in a butcher's shop.'

'Would you walk through the cemetery at midnight?'

'Of course. There's no one here.'

Chapter 9

Kim was in the hut on her laptop, going through a coffee shop training site. She was interested in three courses: setting up a coffee shop, barista training and running a coffee shop. Was barista training worth the £150? She wouldn't be a barista herself, at least she hoped not, but then it would be useful to know what the staff should be doing.

Then the Wi-Fi cut out. How annoying. She was just close enough to the office to pick up theirs, and on a normal day if she lost contact, she would take her chair and laptop outside to get closer, without leaving the stall. But today it was raining, so the hut was her shelter. Going outside would ruin the laptop. Wi-Fi might return in a minute or two, or the rain might stop. Frustrating.

It could well be a waste of time and money attending a course with a provider she knew nothing about. She'd been about to look up customers' criticism when she was cut off. She had a vision of a coffee shop-cum-art gallery. Coffee and paintings, but where and how? Knowing too, she could be dropping money into a big pit and risked losing the lot.

Exciting, she hoped not foolhardy.

The rain was rapping on the roof, a misty veil through the open doorway fading the crematorium and its attendant cars, mourners scurrying into the protection of the building. She gazed at the roadway hypnotically. Legions of droplets splattering on the tarmac, circles sweeping into widening circles in the growing puddles. She could take some photos. A droplet's extinction, striking the water, throwing up a column for the briefest instant, falling and generating circles of ripples. Perhaps a video, in ultra-slow motion, frame by frame. Her own camera was good but not for ultra slow stuff, and anyway, she'd forgotten it today. She'd tried a few shots with her smart phone but they were rubbish.

Rain was so photogenic. So temporary, so grainy. Perhaps in black and white to emphasise the contrast. Scatty not bringing her camera, especially on a day like today, all rain and no customers. And Wi-Fi not working.

Mourners at funerals usually brought their own flowers, big bunches and wreaths. It was visitors to the graves that were her main customers, and they didn't come in this weather. The hut was facing the wrong way, she thought. The obvious thing would be to have the door and windows in front of the stall, so you could see customers coming, see the cars going by. Too obvious for her mother. Perhaps she could see through the walls; it seemed like it sometimes. Though there was a bell on the stall to press for attention.

The awning over the flowers should be bigger, then she could be outside, though she hated Saul watching her, often with his back to her, checking her out through the mirror, and other, bolder times through the window directly. Judging, fantasising. She disliked being on show. Her mother said she should keep an eye on him. Should she be taking pictures of him, like a private eye? Saul salivating, Saul striding out with a clipboard, Saul's visitors, Saul running in from the rain.

Her mother was obsessed with her brother Saul. She and Uncle David were up to something. She'd heard them talking the other day, and they'd moved away when they saw her listening. Something about this afternoon's meeting. Kim was going to be elected onto the board. Money for old rope, said her mother. Five thousand a year for attending a few meetings. She knew it wasn't that simple. The meetings were a family shouting match, everyone leaving with a headache and vowing never to go to another one.

It was supposed to be a two hour session. But Saul could talk non-stop, argue over every full stop and comma, according to her mother. Then the shouting would start, the personal stuff going back ten, twenty, thirty years; the agenda left way behind. There would only be a few non-family members in attendance. How did they put up with it? Why did they?

She'd been dragged in already and had never been to a meeting. Saul had paid her. She was in his pocket. Would be for a while. How long was ten thousand expected to last? Her mother would yell to raise the roof when Kim voted with Saul. She would yell anyway, however she voted. So give her something to yell at.

'Barista Course' or 'Setting Up A Coffee Shop'? She could do both, but if the first was crap she'd be wasting money on the second. Still no Wi-Fi. She must look at customer feed-back.

She was in a ruffled state, trying to block out the meeting ahead and considering courses with insufficient informa-tion, when the car arrived. It drove in fast, stopping in a fierce splash. She was wary of who it might be, hoping it wasn't who she thought. Preparing herself, she placed the laptop under the chair, and stood up. It was chilly, she'd hardly been aware of it while on the net, planning, but she was now. She took her cardigan off the back of the chair and put it on, doing up the buttons one by one deliberately so the car would vanish, the sound of it an illusion.

Trembling, she managed the step or two, and stood in the doorway. Yes, it was he. Trouble. Her legs were instantly hollowed. The visitor was out of the car, slamming the door of the red Jaguar, a tall bald man, in a well cut, expensive grey suit.

'Hello, Kim,' he said. She was sheltered, he was in the rain discomforted by the wetting of his suit. 'Let's go inside,' he added. 'I've something to tell you.'

He gave her little choice as he came forward and would have pushed her out of the way, if she hadn't backed off to let him in. He took the seat nearest the door, forcing her to take the far one. She was trapped.

'Hello, Keith,' she said, brushing her hair back from her forehead.

He was grimacing at the spots of rain on his jacket. Under it he wore a white polo top. He was broad, all the weights he lifted converted to brawn with the assistance of steroids. His skull was shaved to a tanned dome, his teeth white gateways, matching the purity of his polo top.

'He wants to see you,' he said.

She'd guessed this was why he'd come. Why else?

'Brad deceived me from day one,' she managed to say, and could feel her heart thumping in her chest. 'The women I got used to, but when the law caught him and took back all the proceeds of crime...'

'Yeh, that was bad,' admitted Keith, scratching the side of his nose.

'I lost the house, that beautiful garden, my car, status – though I wondered what that was really, arm holder, model, punch bag, whore.'

'You had a good life, Kim. Don't knock it,' Keith insisted. 'Brad gave you it all. What have you got here, three chipped cups and some weeds in pots?' He gave her a broad smile. 'This is not you, Kim sweetheart. You're classier than this. You always had style.'

'I dressed well,' she said. 'That's what money does for you. Pay a designer and stick it on my back.' She reflected. 'But he shut me down, Keith. Wanted me to be his puppet wife. I'm free of him, and that's the way I want to stay.'

'First reaction, babe. I get it. It was a shock,' said Keith, rubbing his hands in the chill. He looked about him, blowing his cheeks. 'You want to get some heat in here. In fact, you want to get out of here completely. This tin pot flower stall.'

Kim could barely see past him, his bulk lodged between her and the outside. There was some sky, smudgy grey, the steeple, a tree branch. How long would he stay?

She said, 'The divorce is going through. This job is temporary. I'm helping my mum out. I have plans. And thinking time while I get them on the move.' She put a hand on Keith's arm. 'Tell Brad I wish him well. I am sorry for all that's happened. But I must go my own way.'

Keith shook her hand off. 'He won't allow it. Not from his wife.' He stood up and grasped her by the shoulders with both hands, digging in with his fingers as he rose above her. 'The divorce has to stop.' He shook her; it didn't hurt but was a warning of what he might do. His hands remained on her shoulder, so close to her neck and breasts. 'Marriage is for life,' he added.

He released her. She sat back in the chair, breathing rapidly. So this was the message. What reply did Brad expect? The terror of those years returned. The beatings and apologies. The fear of saying the wrong word. Watching Brad's mood when he came home.

Keith wiped his hands together. 'You can keep the house, if you play ball.'

'The house is gone,' she said. 'Proceeds of crime, don't they call it?'

'Not the estate. That's gone. But the one round here. Not a palace, but it's got value.'

'It's mine anyway,' she said.

He gripped her shoulders again, squeezing hard. 'It's his. He put it in your name for convenience. All you did was sign on the line.'

She didn't say anything. It wasn't wise to argue, not in this space, by herself.

'There's money too,' he said with a smirk.

'How much?' she said, though without real interest. It was expected of her. Money ruled the clan. But she wasn't going to take a penny.

'A lot,' he said. 'He's got it stashed away. The law never found it. Offshore accounts. You behave, you get it.'

'And if I don't?'

Without warning, Keith slapped her cheek. Her head swung to the side, tears filled her eyes, and in the mist she saw double, slapped into memories, cowering in the bedroom as Brad yelled and hit her.

'Let me think,' she muttered, holding her cheek.

He held her by the chin, squeezing it tightly in his large hand. 'You married into a Catholic family, Kim. Till death do you part. That's the way it goes. One way or another.'

Saying anything would provoke him. Saying nothing would provoke him. This was Brad's brother. Words and silence were attacks.

The stall bell rang. Kim practically leaped out of the chair.

A voice called, 'Hello there. Can I buy some flowers?' Jack appeared at the door. He was in his overalls, very clean after his tidy up at the crematorium. 'I want some for my sister's grave,' he said. 'I'm not sure what's best.'

'Of course, sir.' She rose and strode past Keith to the outside. 'Let me show you what we have.'

She led, Jack followed. She glanced back. Keith had come out and was under the awning. He had to leave her to her customer, though she wondered how Jack knew she was being threatened. Must've heard; Keith was certainly loud.

Now she was outside, she must stay outside. Jack was looking over the flowers quizzically. She saw he was genuinely at a loss. What he wanted, or why he was here.

'We have some nice roses, sir. They last well.'

'I was thinking of a pot plant,' mused Jack looking along the lines of pots. 'Something that would last through the winter. What about these?'

'Primulas,' she said. 'Yes, they flower all winter and burst out in the spring.' She caught Jack's eye. Both knew they were putting on a performance. His wheelbarrow was alongside the hut. Unlikely Keith would know it wasn't there before. He'd been too intent on scaring her. 'Or these double daisies, sir. Then again, a dwarf conifer gives greenery throughout the year. Is there soil on the grave?'

'Yes, there is,' said Jack. 'Full of weeds. But I'm going to take them out. Plant something permanent in her memory.'

'Then go for a dwarf conifer for a feature. It will last twenty years.'

The rain had almost stopped, just a drizzle was falling. Keith was close enough to hear, sheltering to keep the spots off his suit. He picked up a pot plant as if he was considering it, twisting it about in his hands.

'I was wondering about removing the soil altogether,' said Jack.

'You could,' she said. 'Fill the bed with chippings. And have pot plants. Lots to choose from once we get into spring and summer. But you'd have to come back regularly to water them.'

'My brother comes too,' he said. 'So we could keep it up. How about I have those two. What did you call them?'

'Primulas.'

'And this, conifer did you say? And maybe a few roses. Why not? I owe my sister a lot more than that. These chrysanths – do they last well?'

'Very well,' she said, trying not to look at Keith, willing him to go. He was still fingering pot plants, sniffing a red rose. She knew it had no scent.

'Some people say they are bad luck, chrysanths,' said Jack.

'I've never heard that,' she said. 'And I've sold plenty.'

'Dying is bad luck anyway,' said Jack. 'Give me half a dozen. Don't wrap them. I'd only throw the paper away. And the grave's not far. How much do I owe you?'

She calculated, jotting a few figures on a notepad, getting them wrong, her head fuzzy. The calculator was somewhere. Probably inside; she wasn't going in for it. Though it hardly mattered what she said, Keith wasn't going to check, and Jack wasn't really going to pay.

'Nine ninety six,' she said. Can't be right. Too cheap. But she'd said it now.

Jack went through his pockets and handed over a screwed up ten pound note.

'Don't bother with the pennies,' he said, waving away the change.

'Thank you, sir.' She put the note in her money pouch. 'How will you manage this lot?' she added, indicating the collection of pots and cut flowers.

'I could come and go,' he said. 'It's not far.' He pointed out somewhere.

'I'll help you,' she said. 'Keith can look after the stall. Just for a minute or so, eh Keith.' She turned to him and smiled.

Keith glared, and looked at his watch. 'Love to, but I've got to be somewhere. You remember what I said.'

'I certainly will.'

Keith strode to his car, clicking open the door as he approached. He dropped into the bucket seat.

'So shall I tell Brad you'll be visiting?'

'I'll think about it,' she said.

'You do that.'

He slammed the car door as if dismissing her. In a few seconds the car screeched forward, did a half circle and drove back past the flower stall, splashing through the puddles, causing Kim to leap back. Keith put a hand up as he passed without looking at her. Kim watched the car as it continued down the drive and out of the cemetery gates.

Jack too was watching as the Jaguar headed up the road. He was putting the plants back on the shelving.

'Who was he?'

'My soon-to-be ex brother-in-law,' she said, still watching the road, as if the receding car might do an about turn. 'A bastard, as bad as my husband.' She turned to him. 'Thanks for that performance. You must have heard some of what he said.'

'Enough to know it wasn't right,' said Jack. 'I was packing up, thought I'd pop in. And I heard him having a go at you.'

'You played it well,' she said. 'Taking him on would have got you hurt. Here's your tenner back.' She handed the note over and Jack pocketed it. Kim blew out her cheeks. 'Oh, Jack. You sure you want to go out with me?'

'Did he threaten you?' Jack was putting the last rose back in place.

'He told me to stop the divorce or else.'

'Or else what?'

She shook her head, and gave a tight lipped smile. 'You don't want to know, Jack.'

He stared at her, hoping she might add something to mitigate what he feared. But she said no more, holding on to the prop of the awning as if she might fall.

'What are you going to do?' he said.

'I'm not getting involved with that family again. I don't care what happens.'

Chapter 10

It had been a busy morning. Rain or no rain, there was lots to do. Nora had been up in the dark to go to Temple Mills to buy flowers, and then had driven to the cemetery to set up the stall before her daughter Kim arrived. Filling in, so Kim had said. Apparently, her daughter had plans. Plans are easy to have; it's getting on with them that counts. Kim was so lackadaisical, she could barely get up in the morning. Initiative didn't come out of a seed packet.

Kim had been given everything on a plate, and she'd lost the lot. So maybe there was justice in the world.

In the car, outside the office, Nora skimmed the minutes of the meeting. She might not get time later. She'd read them earlier. With meetings every month, you forget, what with the pressure of her own work. Besides which the minutes were expurgated, the invective translated as 'David disagreed' or 'Saul said it was too expensive.' She was impressed with Maureen's prose; the secretary must have wondered what she was doing in a cage of wild animals, but scribbled away and made the evening, in retrospect, seem merely disagreeable. These days, the board meetings were the only time she, David and Saul were in a room together. Ruth would be at the meeting too, family by marriage. Cunning incarnate. She'd got her memorial through when everyone was too exhausted to argue, except David had been so eager to agree, to get one over Saul. Such a silly thing to argue over, a wall and a seat, but then again so much easier to understand than big plans covering years and costing hundreds of thousands of pounds.

She and David had already decided what to do. The meeting would drain them all, no good getting psyched up this early in the day. Though David wanted the two of them to get together beforehand to go over everything. Did she have time? She'd make some one way or another.

She looked in the car mirror. That face didn't get any thinner, the very reverse. At least the mirror couldn't comment on the rest of her body. Ample was what her last boyfriend had said. Meaning only one thing to Eric the snorter. A waste of time, a waste of space, paying for his drug habit. Her hair was bright red, a hint of grey showing at the roots, but only if you pushed the hair back. She'd give it another week before getting it coloured again, cut shorter too, why have gold earrings if no one saw them?

Nora redid her lipstick, touched her face with blusher. She might be getting on but she wouldn't let herself go. Keep smart, look businesslike. Her weight was a problem, diets worked for five minutes, as if to tease you, then yo-yoed back again. Though Japanese seaweed did seem to be working, but was so tasteless. It reminded her of that cellulose filler she'd tried a couple of years ago. It tasted of cardboard and filled you utterly. She'd feel stuffed and bloated all day, like a pregnant hippo.

And there was a size eight, sitting in the chair gazing at nothing. Stop. She must not tell her daughter off. It didn't work. It annoyed Kim, it annoyed herself. And she wanted her vote at the meeting.

'How's it been?' she said brightly, once out of the car and locking up. She adjusted her top and hair.

Kim gave a faint smile. 'It's been quiet, Mum. With the rain. Might pick up now that it's stopped.'

Nora tut-tutted and attacked the pots. 'Have you just been sitting there? You must do the dead-heading, otherwise they look old and we'll just be throwing them out. And that's money down the drain.'

'I did some,' said Kim.

'You didn't do enough,' said her mother sharply. 'The waste has gone through the roof since you took over.' She was picking off the dead flowers in the primula and pansy pots. 'I know you've had problems. Who hasn't? Work is the answer. If you just sit there moping…'

'I am not moping. Please don't start,' she said, holding up both hands to stop the barrage.

'These are too wet,' said Nora, sticking her fingers in the earth of the pots. She wiped her hands with a tissue. 'Over watering kills them. You know that.' She stopped and turned on her daughter who was staring at the ground. 'What have you been doing all morning?'

'I'm filling in. I don't have to do this,' declared Kim. 'I agreed when I came back that I'd help out here. Well, I'm doing it. I am not a florist and don't intend to be. I am making my plans. I just can't rush them.'

'Of course you can't,' snapped her mother.

Kim rolled her eyes. The same old record playing.

'You're like a teenager,' went on Nora. 'Moping around all day, expecting to be waited on hand and foot. You had servants. Well, now you haven't. And I'm not going to keep you. I was out working when I was sixteen. I made my money. Never expected to be kept by my husband. I know you were lady nose-in-the-air with Brad and his pals. Where did that get you?'

'I'm divorcing him. I won't be on your hands much longer.'

'You have plans.'

'Yes.'

'Want to share them?'

'I'm not ready.'

'Tell me when you are.'

Nora was darting about moving pots here and there, pushing vases of flowers forward and back, tidying the wrapping paper. Why did she snap like this? She couldn't stop herself. It was the laziness she saw in her daughter. She couldn't take her simply sitting there, so lifeless. Nora needn't have come to the stall again, could've done more buying and gone straight to the board meeting in a couple of hours. But she didn't trust Kim on her own. And how right she was. The stall could be a nice little earner, but only if you put your heart into it. Kim was treating it like a holiday job.

Nora had had the idea of passing over the flower stall to Kim, and so concentrating on her clothing stalls in various markets. She was already in three, but buying took a lot of her time. Well, it wouldn't be a problem if she could trust Kim to go to the wholesalers to buy the flowers herself. But Kim didn't have a car, and what would she come back with anyway? Perhaps it was a matter of time for her daughter, adjusting, getting over that husband of hers. A bank robbing charmer. Oh, she'd warned her, but of course anything she said, Kim did the opposite.

Things couldn't go on like this, here, at home. She wanted her daughter out. Who wants a daughter in her 30s coming back home? Nora should look for someone to run the stall on a permanent basis. Someone with gumption. She stopped, stood her ground, breathed in and out, counting to herself. Perspective. It was the damned meeting. She was finding fault everywhere. Kim wasn't such a bad girl when you added it up. There were much worse, with drink and drugs, sleeping with god knows who every night. She must keep her mouth shut. She wanted to apologise, but she couldn't. It wasn't in her make up.

'Pack up the stall before the meeting,' said Nora. 'You're going to be voted onto the board early in the meeting. No one will be against it. Just smile and say some nice things about yourself. Nothing negative. Once in, all you have to do is take your cue from me. Vote as I do. Remember that and you won't go wrong. And now I must be off to Romford for the car boot sale. I'll be back for the meeting. Cheer up. It hasn't happened yet.'

And she was back in the car.

Chapter 11

Jack was outside the cemetery, loading the wheelbarrow and tools into his van. He could do nothing more until the footings were dry enough for him to build the wall. So on to Alison's to finish what he'd started in the morning. All he'd done was turn the stopcock off and the electricity. Now he had to find the cause. Most likely the ballcock in the tank. She might not pay him, but then again, he couldn't complain as she'd subbed him often enough when Mia was coming over. He wouldn't ask for money, but if she offered, he'd take it. She could afford it easily enough. He didn't know how much head teachers earned, but a good deal more than he did. And she'd just bought a house. Alison wasn't short of cash.

Jack reflected on the job ahead. Best to get what's needed out now. He leaned in, searching and pulling items aside. A ballcock, various wrenches, a rubber mallet, screwdriver, goggles, gloves. A head torch, it could be dark up in the loft. He put the items into a cloth bag he used for small jobs. He'd noted this morning that Alison had a ladder, so his own could stay in the van. One less bit of gear to cart in.

He hadn't had his lunch yet, so might as well eat at Alison's. In comfort. She always had plenty in, so he could top up. Jack got in the van, and sat back. A breather. The rain had stopped, there was even a little blue in the sky.

That business with Kim. Did he really want to get involved with a woman who was married to a bank robber, even if she was almost divorced? Commonsense said be wary. All he'd committed himself to was seeing a house and dinner. What would Maria be doing tonight? Who had she been seeing between times? Just as well he was going out with Kim; he wouldn't be sitting at home feeling sorry for himself. Always the danger that he'd head for the bottle. He really should get back to Alcohol Halt, talk to his mentor, Max. He was getting stressed again. Getting things out of proportion.

Would it always be like this? Year on year, into middle age, short term relationships, into old age, and dying alone. Max had cautioned him on pessimism. Some long relationships were awful, nigh on impossible to get out of. Value your freedom. Jack grinned at the thought. Momentarily free, and eager to be enchained again. *Love is a four letter word*. A Max quote.

Time to get to Alison's. He was hungry.

His phone rang, the distinctive ring of a text coming in. He looked. It was from Maria. Should he read it? Silly thought, how could he not?

Sorry to be so harsh. I'm not sure any more.

He almost wept, almost died laughing, leaning backwards, eyes to the roof. This was all he needed. A maybe, a half possibility. What was she playing at? She knew he'd respond. He was a rat in a maze; he'd press the button and this time get no reward. So he would keep pressing it, in the vain hope of one.

Another text came. He knew it'd be her. She could send seven in a row. Why couldn't she just phone him? But then he didn't want her phoning, unsure what she'd say, what he'd say in return.

Let's meet and talk about us.

He didn't want to. No way.

He texted back: *When and where?*

There, he'd said, more or less, that he'd meet her. Then what? Maybe their relationship would be back on. He sensed though that whatever happened, it was on the skids. Forget it. He looked up at the sky. The clouds were clearing rapidly.

He'd like to get out with the telescope instead of waiting on texts. Better than sex on a fine night, he sometimes joked. Though a breeze that blew clouds away, could blow more in. There were times he'd set his telescope up on a starry evening, and, by the time he was ready for viewing, the sky was covered.

And there was Kim of course. He was seeing her tonight.

No reply from Maria. She could be so swift, tap-tapping with busy fingers. Maybe she was regretting sending the first couple.

Jack set off to Alison's, turning on the player at the song he'd been listening to in the morning, Glen Campbell's *Wichita Lineman:* a lovesick guy working alone, fixing the endless stretch of phone lines out on the prairie, expecting snow. It had been apt coming into work, the aftermath of Maria's dismissal. Great self pity music. Even now, the music schmoozed him as he drove. For a minute or two, he was under a huge sky, heartbroken and cold, up a telephone pole mending the line.

Jack parked outside Alison's and listened to the end of the song. It ached with loneliness, the guy miles from anywhere, up a phone pole, and getting no messages.

Pathetic.

Great song though.

He switched off the player, took up the tool bag and got out of the van. He locked up and, while heading up Alison's path, checked he had her key. Yes, still in his pocket. Here comes the Forest Gate Lineman. He'd do the repair job, have some lunch. And stop daydreaming.

Jack opened the front door and heard a fridge door slam from inside the house. That was odd. There wasn't supposed to be anyone in. Mia was at school, Alison at work. Mia had been in trouble about six months ago for bunking off. Not at it again? He was here to fix the plumbing, not bawl his daughter out. Jack closed the door as quietly as he could, and crept down the hallway to the kitchen.

There, sitting at the kitchen table, was an Asian girl. She was eating a bowl of salad and beans and was obviously startled to see him. She was slight, her black hair tied back in a ponytail. She wore jeans and a dirty blue T-shirt, a backpack lying on the table.

'Who are you?' he said.

'A friend,' she said, staring at him with cavernous black eyes. She'd stopped eating.

Jack meditated; Alison hadn't said anything about anyone being here. The girl certainly hadn't been here first thing when he'd turned off the water.

'Whose friend?' he said.

'The girl. I'm her friend.'

'What girl? What's her name?'

'I've forgotten.' She grimaced to recall, snapping her fingers. 'Mia. She said it was OK.'

'Did her mum say it was OK?'

'She did. I stayed overnight. I'm just having a bite to eat then I'm going.'

'Shouldn't you be at school?'

'Teachers' training today.'

'What school you at?'

'Sarah Bonnell. You know, in Stratford.'

He knew the school; it was Mia's. And Mia was at school as far as he knew, so how could there be a training day? Though lying wasn't out of the question for Mia. She could have taken advantage of the day off to do her own thing. Whatever that might be. Or was this girl lying? Would Alison leave a girl in the house on her own? Had she been here all along when he'd come this morning, in bed?

She was finishing the bowl quickly.

He said, 'Did you get up with Mia this morning?'

'Yes. I slept in her room.' She'd finished the bowl. She rose. 'Must go now.'

'Put the bowl in the dishwasher before you go.'

'Of course.' She searched along the unit, Jack purposely didn't help. Finding the dishwasher, she pulled down the door, pulled out the tray and put in the bowl and her fork.

While she was doing so, Jack had taken up the backpack. He shook the contents onto the table. She turned as she heard the rattle on the wooden surface. A laptop, jewellery, a watch and headphones tumbled out. Jack recognised some of the items. He'd given the watch to Mia, the laptop was Mia's too, the brooch was Alison's.

'How dare you!' exclaimed the girl. 'That's my stuff.'

'The watch belongs to Mia,' he said.

'She gave it to me.'

'And the laptop?'

'I'm borrowing it.'

Her face was screwed up, she was so thin.

'And the brooch?'

'Mia's mum gave it to me.'

Jack laughed at her weak defence. Though she wasn't giving in.

'You're a thief and a liar,' he said. He took out his phone.

'You phoning the police?'

'I'm phoning Sarah Bonnell. Checking whether today is a teachers' training day.'

'Don't bother,' she said with a shrug. 'It isn't.'

The girl had sat down at the table. Her arms were so skinny. Tough but vulnerable. He had no doubt she was a burglar. But what was he going to do with her?

'How old are you?'

'Seventeen.'

'Too old for Sarah Bonnell.'

'It was my school,' she said. 'And I do know Mia. She's in year 8...' She reflected, 'No, year 9 now. Smart girl. Good at science and maths.'

'None of which explains the gear in your bag,' said Jack. 'I was here this morning around nine o'clock. And you weren't. So how did you get in?'

She didn't reply, staring at him, an angry arrogance, almost as if he were in the wrong. He was between her and the door, knowing she'd make a break for it if she could.

'Tell me the truth or I'm going to call the police.'

'You mean, you might not?'

'I haven't decided. What's your name?'

'Chitra.'

'Where do you live?'

She shrugged. 'Here and there. Depends.'

'You're not living at home?'

'No way.'

'Why not?'

'My stepfather's a pig. He raped me. I told my mum. She told me not to tell anyone or call the police. So I left home.'

Jack was unsure what to do. She could be telling the truth. She could be telling a pack of lies. Either way she was a thief, but her stepfather's behaviour, if true, was some mitigation.

'Why this house?' he said.

'The garden backs on to the railway,' she said. 'I went along the cutting and just picked this place. I climbed over the back fence. That kitchen door is too easy to open.' She indicated the door disparagingly. 'Look at that lock. Pathetic. It's only on a Yale. Easy to pick. You going to call the cops?'

'How did you know Mia lived here?'

'I saw a photo of her in the living room, realised I knew her from school.' She shrugged. 'That's all.'

She was telling the truth now. There was a photo of Mia in the sitting room on the sideboard. And how she got in rang true. The back door had two locks but Alison only used the flimsier one.

'Put the kettle on,' he said.

'Why?'

'We'll have a coffee. While I have a think what to do with you.'

Chapter 12

Saul parked his car outside the office. Each day at noon exactly, he'd stop work and go home to pick up Sarah, his wife. Maureen would cope while he was out. Sumitra came in to the office three days a week for the accounts but today wasn't one of her days.

It was the routine that had attracted him to the funeral business. His first job had been in sales, selling plastics machinery: extruders and injection moulders. On the road, going to factories and finding Mr X was never in, or too busy. When you did get to see Mr X there were competitors undercutting you, and even those jobs you thought you had in the bag, at the last moment the customer found a better deal. Or thought they had. Cowboys competing with cowboys, often selling the same Japanese machine and cutting their margins.

His father had worked at the cemetery, buying a share cheaply from the old man who'd liked him. And over time, his father bought up more and brought his sons in as he gained more control on the board. A straightforward business, at least it had been, you worked regular hours, a plot of earth was a plot of earth. You don't bamboozle people with rates of flow and computer controls, no soft soaping over long lunches, laughing at unfunny jokes. Or rather, that had been the practice when he'd joined the business. A little sloppy but enough for everyone. Then came the rise of the funeral chains. They were the sharpest of dealers, who could force the margins, playing off this cemetery with the City of London or Woodgrange, both less than a mile away. It had been gentlemanly when he'd begun, now it was more cutthroat by the year. The way of the world.

He was trying to keep his mind off the meeting. But he couldn't. Nora and David were up to something. Was Ruth in on it? He had been able to get on with her at least, except with this stupid memorial business. It would've been better to keep her on side. He dreaded the meetings, they wound him up, the family conspired. He knew they'd been meeting outside, planning. They'd get him shouting and ranting, David would be up on his high horse, Nora would pretend to mediate. How long would they be at it this time? The cemetery shut, the office walls quaking with anger.

Don't rehearse. Wait.

Saul removed the folded wheelchair from the boot of the car. He unfolded it and wheeled it to the rear passenger door which he opened. Sarah was on the back seat with her carer, Badrah. Badrah was in her 30s, a Muslim woman, wearing a hijab and a long dress. She was one of five carers to cover the days and most evenings. Sarah passed the cushion to Saul. He placed it on the seat of the wheelchair. He then lifted Sarah out; she clung round his neck, her legs hanging heavily as he placed her. Always a weight but he had the knack, knowing where to put the wheelchair so as to swing her onto it. He put her feet on the step, and made sure the cushion was snug underneath her. Badrah passed him the blanket, gloves and laptop computer. Saul eased the blanket over Sarah's knees and folded it in at the sides. He put the computer on her lap and secured it with two straps to both armrests. An earlier model had fallen off while Saul was pushing the chair, breaking the laptop, hence this adaptation. Sarah put on the gloves herself, a light pair of fingerless gloves. Autumn could be chilly.

Badrah now had a break in her day, though it was too far for her to go home; Saul and Sarah would only be gone for half an hour. When newly in the post Badrah, being free, had gone into the office to talk to Maureen. Only once, as Saul had admonished her for distracting his assistant, who wasn't paid to gossip. Today Badrah went over to Kim at the flower stall. No objections to that, as Kim was never that busy and there was usually a cup of tea for her.

Sarah wore a long blue dress, the bottom half covered in the blanket. Round her neck was a red and blue silk scarf with a pattern of hummingbirds. She had a number of scarves and picked which to wear each time she came to the cemetery. On her feet, she wore red slip-ons, decorative more than anything as she couldn't stand. Her hair had gone grey soon after the accident but a hairdresser came to the house once a month. She dyed Sarah's hair a deep brown and kept it short and in good order. Sarah did her own make-up, taking her time over it, but that was no matter, provided Saul allowed for it when he went out with her. Sarah became very anxious if he tried to hurry her along.

She'd kept her looks into middle age, and with her make-up and scarf was colourful and attractive. She couldn't speak but would write on the laptop which would then speak the words she'd written in a flat, very posh voice. Sarah was slow at the keyboard, as she'd developed arthritis in her wrists and hands, and could become frustrated at her thwarted communication.

Saul began their walk.

'I thought we wouldn't get out today, dear,' he said, 'what with the rain, but it stopped just in time.'

Sarah nodded, tight lipped, a hint of a smile.

Saul wheeled her over to the flower stall. Kim and Badrah were there.

Kim said, 'Hello, Sarah,' in a somewhat exaggerated voice. 'That's a lovely scarf you're wearing.'

Sarah tapped a few buttons on the laptop. It replied haltingly: 'Hello, Kim. Beautiful display today.' Certain words and phrases were pre-programmed. This was a regular walk.

'The primulas and pansies are very colourful,' said Kim. 'Have you seen my mum today?'

Sarah tapped a button. 'No.'

Saul stood by stiffly, like a museum attendant, while his wife and niece were speaking. He'd promised Kim a lot of money earlier. Could he trust her? He should've said half now, half after. Too late for that. Nothing he could say to her with Sarah here. All these deals, plotting. He should be a Trappist monk, silent, obedient, a slave to routine. No meetings, no talking, the only voice the one in his head.

'We'll head on, dear,' he said. 'We'll see Kim again when we come back.'

'See you soon,' said Kim.

'See you soon,' said the laptop.

Saul pushed on. The walk was a routine, with all stations visited in its circuit. Beginning with the flower stall. Sarah wanted it that way, became agitated if he missed a place. It was her walk. For this daily half-hour, he had her to himself. Sarah had been prepared for it, been taken to the toilet before leaving the house, chosen her silk scarf, put her make-up on and the red slip-ons. It was a ritual. He was needed, no one in his way.

'I do like the autumn,' he said. 'The nip in the air and the squirrels. But there's so much clearing up to do with all the conkers and fallen leaves.'

They went on a little way before the computer said, 'I like conkers.'

'We'll pick some up on our way, shall we?' he said, 'but first we'll visit Jack Cornwell.'

Jack Cornwell was the celebrity of the cemetery. His grave was a squarish marble column with a flower bed in front. Against the sides were wreaths from last Remembrance Day, the next was due in a month. The boy hero had been a 16-year-old gunner on a battleship who lied about his age to get into the navy. In 1916, he was mortally wounded at the Battle of Jutland and given a posthumous Victoria Cross for remaining at his station.

'Did the lad have any idea what he was doing?' said Saul.

He patiently awaited Sarah's reply, not rushing her as she tapped out the words, though he more or less knew what she would say. He wanted to kiss her. She tried so hard.

'Going on an adventure,' said Sarah's laptop.

The memorial always held them. Saul grieved the boy who had become famous once dead. It seemed the ultimate unfairness. Saul wanted him to know he was honoured.

'Poor kid,' said the laptop.

He wheeled her on, down the avenue named after the hero of Jutland. Conkers and leaves had been swept away in the morning, but were falling again. A horse chestnut fell ahead of them, hitting the tarmac and splitting open, spilling the conker.

'Conker, please,' said Sarah's machine.

Saul picked up the fresh one and a couple more. He put them in her hand, folding her fingers over them. She opened her palm and rubbed one like a precious stone. He gathered a few more for her, the perfect ones, as sometimes the skins were cracked where they struck the tarmac. He placed them in a line along the edge of her computer. His gift.

'It's going to be terrible this afternoon,' he said. 'David and Nora have something up their sleeve. I know it. I don't know whether Ruth is in on it.'

'Not now,' said the laptop.

'Quite right,' said Saul. 'It's no help.'

Sarah was on the board nominally, but she never came to the meetings. She had once but found it too stressful as she was unable to engage, felt patronised, and decided to never go again.

They stopped by the fallen angel, the third station of their walk. Her head had cracked off when she fell from her plinth. Saul had had her moved to the yard to be taken away, but next time round Sarah had demanded that she be put back. And so she was, Sarah directing exactly how she was to lie.

The head was that of a young girl, a visage of ecstasy. Her angelic body lay belly up, hands together in prayer, though the fingertips had broken off. She wore a dress down to her small bare feet. There were wings on her back which raised her headless torso higher than her feet. Saul had suggested re-attaching the head but Sarah wouldn't have it. The statue was broken and should stay broken. Perhaps symbolic of themselves. Their marriage had been close to breaking before the accident. She'd been planning to leave him.

'You are the only person I trust,' he said.

He kneeled down before her, his head just above her knees. She clasped his face. He took a hand and kissed the fingers, gently biting a tip, tears welling.

'My dear, I am so sorry,' he said. His second apology that day, perhaps both for the same thing, for his unrequited sexual fantasies, for his love.

She closed her eyes and leaned her head back, face to the sky. Saul felt the sob through her hands.

Chapter 13

Jack was eating his lunch at Alison's. He'd let the girl go. And once he'd made that decision, he'd allowed her to take some food with her in a plastic box. As she was leaving, he gave her a ten pound note. Chitra was only a couple of years older than Mia, and surely had problems even if only half of what she'd told him was true. She was hardly more than a child and there had to be a painful back story.

For his own lunch, Jack had made at home only a couple of cheese sandwiches but Alison had a well stocked fridge. He helped himself to some tuna salad. He was finishing off with a fruit yogurt and coffee when his phone rang. He took it out of his pocket.

Maria. Did he even want to talk to her? And then he answered the phone in panic, in case the ringing should stop.

'Hello, Maria.'

'Hello, Jack. I thought a few words would be in order.'

He sometimes chided her for her bookish language, but not this time.

'I was surprised to get your text,' he said.

'Which one?'

'The one last night knocked me for six. But the recent ones too. I'd assumed it was all over between us. I wasn't expecting a rethink.'

'I don't want anyone else to get you.'

He laughed. 'Fat chance,' he said, not wanting to mention Kim which might lead anywhere or nowhere.

'I couldn't sleep last night,' she said.

'Good.'

'I was wondering what you thought of me.'

'And not the effect your text might have had on me?'

'That too.'

It seemed an afterthought.

'Have you got someone else?' he said.

There was a pause before she said, 'Can we meet and talk about things?'

'Let's not spoil a good dinner.'

'Ouch.' He wasn't unhappy at the strike. 'I only meant food should be enjoyed,' she went on, 'not quarrelled over.'

'That still applies.'

'You could come to my place at five thirty.'

This was tricky. He was meeting Kim at 6.30. But then it might be useful to have to leave Maria. It would stop pussy-footing if he had to leave early. Give him an advantage. But not her place.

'Make it West Ham Park,' he said. 'The Iris Garden.'

'It'll be wet.'

'Bring your umbrella.' He rang off.

If it was important to her, then she'd come. If a wet bench worried her too much, then their relationship wasn't worth a light. He wondered what new things she had to say. It suddenly hit him. She was pregnant. First she didn't want to see him, then she did. It all fitted. She hadn't wanted to tell him on the phone. Would she keep it or have an abortion? Might there be two mothers he had a long term relationship with?

Heaven help him.

He was jumping to conclusions. It could be a host of things, other than pregnancy. A new lover, an old lover, something from her past, just doubts about him and her. Wait to be told, don't presume. He got attached too quickly, that was his trouble. Take it step by step. Maria had something to say. Perhaps she wanted a looser set up. Or she wanted to be tied up, or have him tied up? Don't go screaming into panic mode.

And then there was Kim. A dinner, that's all. He'd made her no promises. Had he told her he was not in a relationship? He thought he had. Well, it'd been true at the time, was still true. Might not be when they met. Or might be.

Uncertainty ruled.

He finished his lunch and tidied up. Alison would not appreciate coming back to a mess. He was much tidier at the home of customers than he was in his own place. Even if Alison was going to balance this off against past favours, he should give her nothing to complain about.

Jack took his tools upstairs. Alison's step-ladder was in a recess on the landing. He took it into the bathroom and set up the ladder under the trap door in the ceiling. He climbed, pushed the flap open. There was a light switch. He flipped it, but it didn't go on, only then recalling he'd disabled the lights this morning as water was dripping through the light fittings.

He sorted out his head torch. With it on his forehead, he climbed into the loft. The space was large, going over the upper rooms, and had floorboards over the joists which made life easier. There wasn't much here, no doubt because it was too difficult to get to. A few suitcases, dusty cardboard boxes, and the water tank, a large metal cube, the sides about a metre long and high.

Looking into the tank, he saw the ballcock had sunk. So this was the culprit. It should be floating on the water, gradually shutting off the inlet as the water level rose, but it had a hole in and so was full of water. Useless. In a few minutes, he took off the broken ballcock and replaced it with the one he'd brought along.

In his morning visit, he'd shut off the water coming into the house to stop the flooding. Jack climbed down the ladder and went downstairs to the front door and turned the stopcock back on. He checked in the kitchen; the cold tap whooshed and spurted, and then ran freely.

Something though was bothering him.

He went upstairs, he climbed back into the loft. The tank had an overflow pipe. What should have happened, when the ballcock stopped working, was that excess water should have run out through the overflow pipe. The pipe went through the wall of the house, and any overflow should have streamed into the front garden, and not been spilling over the top of the tank and through the ceiling.

He found the overflow outlet in the side of the tank. It was just below the water level. Excess water should be flowing out. It had to be blocked. Jack put a finger in and prodded. There was something in there. He inched about, thinking he might have to push it right through the pipe with his screwdriver, though that risked jamming it even more. There was something leathery, flexible. Jack scraped at it with his nail. It was coming, and then a stringy piece was poking through and he was able to tug at it. It wouldn't come, so he gave a sharp tug and it came out of the pipe into his hands.

Jack was holding a grey mouse by the tail. And heavens! it was moving, the tiny legs scrabbling in the air, the body curling up on itself to where Jack was holding it. He dropped the mouse; it fell to the floor, landing on its feet. It lay there an instant as if catching its breath, legs wriggling, ears twitching. How long had it been stuck in the pipe? Lucky not to have drowned.

The mouse crawled off. Not a rapid, panicky motion, perhaps because it was stiff from its confinement. Sluggishly, it made its way into the shadows at the edge of the loft and was lost in the darkness.

Water was gurgling out of the overflow. As it should be. He stayed in the loft until it ceased. New ballcock, the overflow unblocked, job done. He wondered about the mouse getting into the pipe. Once in, it must have forced its way further in until it was stuck. He felt sorry for the animal and searched the eaves but couldn't find it, nor any blood, so maybe the animal wasn't badly hurt.

Jack tidied everything away, remembering to turn the upstairs lights back on at the fuse box. He went downstairs to the kitchen and made himself a cup of tea. The plaster in the ceiling was stained and bulging. More work for a builder.

Mia came in. He would have left maybe an hour before she was due but the long chat with Chitra delayed him. His daughter had a stuffed backpack of books. There always seemed way too many. So much to learn. Or, as had been his case, not to learn. He couldn't wait to leave school and get away from the teachers demanding he know this and that, without any reason for it.

'I see you fixed the leak, Dad.'

She was neatish in her school uniform of a white shirt and navy trousers.

'It's all back to normal,' he said.

She grinned. 'Mum was panicking this morning. As I was leaving for school, she was gabbing to you on the phone.'

Mia went to the fridge and poured herself some orange juice. She was tall and slim, her figure was filling out. What troubles lay ahead? Her hair was tied back in a ponytail, some of which was coming out of the band.

'Did you know a girl called Chitra?' he said.

She'd sat down with him at the table with her glass of juice.

'There was a Chitra at school,' said Mia. 'Left some time last year. She played the trumpet and was good at football. I liked her. Why you asking?'

He wondered what to tell her.

'Don't tell your mum,' he said. And then told her about finding Chitra in the house, when he came to do the repair, and what he'd done.

'You sure you got it all back from her?' exclaimed Mia.

'I emptied her bag,' he said. 'Anything else would have to be small.'

Mia screwed up her face. 'I'm going upstairs to look.'

She ran off.

He hoped nothing of hers was taken. Or Mia would have a go at him. And most definitely, he would not tell Alison about Chitra and risk her wrath at letting the girl go.

PART TWO:
THE FAMILY MEETING

Chapter 14

Kim was closing the flower stall. There were a few hours to go before the cemetery shut but she was due at the meeting. Mr Greene, the solicitor, had already arrived. Auntie Ruth had come, and chatted with Kim, saying she didn't want to go in early as she'd be stuck talking to Saul. She'd wait until a few more arrived. Ruth was blonde, in her 50s, thin rather than slim. She dressed well but Kim always thought she wore too much make-up for too little effect. Not something she would ever tell her.

Kim kept working as Ruth chatted on, talking about the weather and the cruise she'd booked over Christmas. She ran a catering company, the Little Catering Company, which was why she'd kept her single name, Little, instead of being another Coe. The company specialised in weddings, and at Christmas she could get away for a couple of weeks.

'I should get up and see how my builder is getting on,' said Ruth.

'He's put the footings in,' said Kim.

'Oh, so you know about footings, do you? Been chatting up the builder, have you?' she said with a wink.

Uncle David arrived, coming over from the crematorium, and Ruth and he chatted, deliberately going some distance away from Kim so she couldn't overhear. What were they saying that was so important, she wondered.

All the flowers had to go in the hut, along with trowels, watering can, wrapping paper and so forth. Nothing to be left out. It had been hardly worth her coming in today with all the rain. Ten customers at most, plus a telling off from her mother. Though she'd booked places on two courses:

'Setting up a Coffee Shop' and 'Barista Training'. Why not, with the money coming in from Uncle Saul. Splash out, risk it. She must get on the move, not wanting to work at the flower stall any longer than necessary. Her mother had made it a condition for her moving back home. At first it had been OK. The work gave her a timetable, allowed her to get her head straight after the disaster when Brad was arrested, when she'd lost virtually everything as proceeds of crime. Nothing was in her name, except the one house. And now she had to access it, and she had Jack in attendance to look it over. That was rather cheeky of her, then again she was taking him out to dinner afterwards. And they wouldn't be long going round the house. A quick look to get the feel of the place.

The flower stall, which had been welcome at first, getting her up in the morning, had become tedious. Imagine doing it forever! Her mother needed a permanent worker, someone who wanted to do it, though the snag was that anyone who was any good wouldn't stay.

Not her problem. She wasn't staying either.

Mr Boyd, the company secretary, drove up. Alighting from his car, he gave her a quick wave and went straight in. David and Ruth, who had been talking conspiratorially, saw there was sufficient inside to dilute Saul, and decided they could enter themselves. Through the window, Kim could see the central table set up, with papers and glasses of water. Maureen, she knew, would be taking the minutes.

Her mother arrived, driving in too fast. She came over to the stall, breathing heavily, not complaining for once. She said she must go straight in and check any new papers before the meeting began.

'Just follow my lead when it comes to the vote,' said Nora.

Kim nodded and said she'd be in as soon as she could. She watched her mother go into the office, always in a hurry, amazing the energy she had considering her weight. She hoped she wouldn't go that way herself as she slipped into middle age. But she certainly wouldn't be following her mother's lead on the vote. Why should she? They'd manipulated to get her on the board, and now expected her to tamely follow their prodding. Ten thousand pounds was somewhat dishonourable but why would David make a better Chair than Saul? She'd take the money and her mother's wrath, which she had anyway, and get her plans on the move.

A couple more arrived who she didn't know. They both ignored her, not realising she was family, assuming she was a nobody, a flower girl at a stall. Such things gave her a dig in the esteem. She wanted to shout out: *I'm going on the board! I've got ten thousand pounds*. She smiled; they'd find out soon enough.

Kim had fallen from grace on coming back, become a manual worker, when she'd been the lady of the manse. With a cook, a cleaner, a gardener, along with her unfaithful, lying, gangster husband. Well, it was time to move on. She'd got over the devastation of Brad's arrest and trial. All she'd needed was cash. She had the shares she'd inherited in the cemetery giving her interest, not enough for her schemes, but now the ten thou from Saul, and there was the house of unknown value. It was a sign. She'd been rich, married to a rich crook, had her hair done too often, shopping till she dropped, coming home to an empty house where more than once she'd considered slashing her wrists.

Her time was coming.

Kim had resisted going on the board. She hadn't realised there was money in it, for just attending. Everyone thought she knew. She hadn't. Once she had, she'd agreed. She could stomach a family row every few months. It was essential she toughen up if she was going to run her own business. And who knows, the cemetery could be an opportunity. With everyone against everyone, might she not find herself in demand?

The family controlled 60% of the shares and so were in control. Or rather, would be if they worked together. There'd be a bust up today. Then a grand row between her and her mother. Just as well, it would push her to leave home. Her mother had made it clear she didn't want her there, and she herself didn't want to be there. Nora could stick her flower stall. The courses began in ten days. Kim was on her way. Taking control.

Chapter 15

The bench was wet, but Jack had brought a cloth. He wiped the seat, and stuffed the damp cloth in his overalls pocket. Dry enough for him, though Maria might gripe. He looked at his watch. The agreed time. He was there, if she wasn't.

The Iris Garden in West Ham Park was part of the larger ornamental garden. The irises, when in bloom, were outnumbered by an assortment of plants, some flowering and many leafy in the shade of the high plane trees. He and Maria had come here in early summer when they were first going out and seen the irises, like blue turkey heads. All that was left of them were the sausage-like rhizomes growing lumpily on the earth, and their long leaf blades. Maria had pointed out to him the sage and the alliums with their prickly-ball heads, much of which Jack forgot, or pretended to, and had to be reminded every visit.

Today, the leaves were thinning in the trees overhanging the garden. The tennis court was hidden by a shrub hedge, present only in the thwack of balls. Ahead, over a low hedge, was the bandstand. He and Maria had come to a jazz concert one Sunday afternoon and afterwards spread a cloth on the grass for a picnic. It had been a summer romance. This was its autumn.

And then she was there, in a black waterproof jacket, zipped up to the neck, jeans and trainers. On her head, she wore a woolly tam o'shanter, flat as a discus, but quite fetching in its red and green, her straw blonde hair spilling out the sides. She'd put on make-up; her scent as she sat down made him weak at the knees. He mustn't give in to her. It was she who'd wanted to end things; it was she who had changed her mind.

'Hello, Jack.'

No hug, a telling gap between them on the bench.

'This place is looking tired,' he said. Like he was, he could've added, the lack of sleep catching up with him. 'I have to leave in half an hour,' he added, looking at his watch.

'A deadline,' she said. 'I should have typed out my thoughts, given you a sheet to peruse and sign.'

'I don't know what you want,' he said. 'Maybe I never did.' He turned to her. 'What's changed?'

'Me,' she said.

He waited. They were like statues, hardly looking at each other. He was observing the leaves in the high branches ahead, burnt and crisp, the green squeezing out of them.

'I think I'm bisexual,' she said. 'Correction,' she added, 'I am bisexual. I get the best of both worlds.'

Or the worst, he thought.

'I met someone at work,' she went on, 'another nurse. She's bi too but in an open relationship.'

'What's an open relationship?'

'It means you can include others.'

'How long have you been seeing her?'

'A few weeks.'

That hurt. He recognised it as jealousy, childish and possessive. Had Maria been in his bed thinking of someone else? He thought so. Why else send last night's text?

'Are you suggesting we have the same?' he said. 'An open relationship.'

'Yes,' she said. She turned to him for the first time, a face he knew but didn't know, as selfish and as greedy as he was. She had dimpled cheeks, a softness belying her power. 'We simply admit who we are,' she went on, 'not monogamous, but with more needs than one person can satisfy.'

'Not so fast,' he said. 'I'm jealous already.'

She moved closer and took his hand. 'That's to be expected. At first. But then, with time, it will be part of our lives.'

'But we'd be less available for each other.'

She smiled and shrugged. 'That can't be helped. When you are with me I shan't ask you about any other relationships, and ditto you me.' She opened her hands wide, expressing freedom. 'So no guilt, no cheating, no lies.'

'Why doesn't everyone do it?' he said.

'Too wound up. Too puritanical. Too possessive, living a life of lies. Pretending they don't fancy other people when they do like mad. We would be admitting it.'

She was making it sound something other than selfish, noble even. But he was sure she simply wanted more sex. Variety.

'Do you prefer men or women?' he said, thinking of the mysterious nurse, already in competition with him.

'Men,' she said, kissing her index finger and planting it on his lips. But he guessed if she were with the nurse, she'd have said women. It wasn't an end to lies. You made peace with whom you were with.

'So are you game?' she said.

'I'll have to think about it.'

She sprang up, took a couple of steps away and pointed back at him.

'Think about it as long as you like. But I might not be here.'

'Maria!'

But she was striding away, over the flagstones. She turned back for an instant and prodded the air between them.

'I thought you were more adventurous, Jack, but I was wrong. You're a stick in the mud.'

And she was out of the iris garden. A woman in a hijab across the garden was staring at him, trying to make sense of Maria's parting shot, as he was himself. Part of him wanted to chase after her. And say what? That he still did not know what he wanted. That it was true, he was a stick in the mud. He hadn't climbed the North Face of the Eiger or sailed single-handed across the Atlantic. He was a builder, one drink away from a drunk. He was one of those she despised. What had she called them? Wound up, puritanical, possessive. All of them applied.

He saw himself chasing after her, saying he would play the game, but knew that he could not convince her. He had to say yes, with so much passion the flagstones would leap in the air. But that wasn't the way of stick in the muds. And he knew that she could only hurt him. He would never be adventurous enough.

Nor was it over.

Jack stayed in the garden, on the bench, deflated. She wasn't pregnant. Might that have been better? Tied her to him, or he to her, for better or worse. Did he love her? Whatever that meant. She had kicked him in the manhood, challenged him and he wasn't up to it. He would see her again, but when, how, he didn't know. He imagined knocking on her door and she coming down naked under a dressing gown, disturbed in the act of sex. That was the way it would be. Join the queue. Make appointments. What on earth was he going to do? He was supposed to be meeting Kim in half an hour. He should go home and change.

But he couldn't move.

Chapter 16

'What were you playing at?' yelled David.

They were in the office. He was standing between Kim and the outside door, blocking her way. In that mood, she wouldn't try pushing past him. Her mother was on the other side of the counter, talking to Ruth too loudly.

'I wasn't playing at anything,' Kim said quietly.

David shook a fist. 'Why do you think we got you on the board?'

'So I'd do your bidding, Uncle David. Be obedient. Well, I'm sorry. I couldn't see any point in change. Tweedle Dee or Tweedle Dum. At least I know how Tweedle Dee is doing. But you just started yelling, without saying how you'd be any better than Uncle Saul. Insulting him but no programme. How could you expect me to vote for that?' She stopped to take a breath, and then thought of something incontestable. 'I was thinking of Aunty Sarah; she depends on Saul.'

'You did it to spite me!' yelled her mother, leaning across the counter as if she would leap over it in spite of her size. 'There's an ungrateful daughter.' She looked to Ruth and David for confirmation. 'When your father left, I took on the burden, did I complain? And how do you repay me?'

'It makes no sense,' exclaimed David, leaning against the door, knowing there was no way past him. 'The numbers were for us. We had him by the throat.'

He stepped towards her as if he would slap her. Kim stood her ground. She would be slapped if needs be, then knee him in the crotch. He stopped a foot from her, his face pure anger with flecks of white spit on his lips.

'I've always been on your side, Kim. Defended you against your mother. Believe me, I have. I said you were more than a gangster's moll. You were family. You would come good in time.'

'Please don't go on about family, David,' said Ruth wearily. She was leaning against the table which was littered with the papers of the meeting. 'You wanted to depose your brother,' she went on, 'so not much family feeling there.' She turned to Kim. 'I know why you did it, dear. It's obvious. He bought you, like a common whore. No point denying it. You could have abstained, you could have voted with us, but you went with Saul. Money changed hands. I hope it was a lot because you are most certainly going to regret this.'

'Thank you very much, aunty. I value your support.' Kim was working to hold back her tears, blinking rapidly. She looked at her watch as if she had an important appointment. 'Much as I have enjoyed this family get together, I do have to be away, so if you have anything else to say, say it now.'

She would not bow down. Or break into tears. Let them say it all. She would stand her ground. After all, what could they do to her? The three of them. David on his own would alarm her, but with the three to witness each other, all that they had was noise.

'I want you out of my house! Tonight!' yelled Nora. 'I let you come back in exchange for support, for daughterly assistance. Much you know about that, you little bitch. You two-timing guttersnipe. Pack your bags. Go back to your gangsters!'

'I assume I get the day off from the flower stall tomorrow,' said Kim with mock pleasantness. 'I was so looking forward to another day of extreme boredom. I expect you've nothing more important than to run it your-self.'

'I'll do the stall tomorrow,' said Ruth. 'I know you've got a lot on, Nora.'

'Thank you so much, Ruth. I'm up to my ears. And now I've got to find someone reliable.' She sighed, much put upon. 'But it was only a matter of time. Kim has plans of her own, you know. She was just filling in, doing me a favour. I'm sure Uncle Saul will assist with her plans. Why don't you ask him to put you up this evening, dear?'

She pressed her eyes shut, to halt the tears. No, she couldn't. She took a step forward.

'If you'll be kind enough to move, Uncle David, I want to leave.'

Then it came, the slap she'd been expecting but had assumed its time was past. She found it not so easy to knee someone in the crotch once you are reeling. You have to be swift, you have to be ready. Better too, if your opponent is not twice your size.

David was holding out a handkerchief to her as she turned about and lifted the counter board. Her mother and Ruth did not impede her as she strode across the room, though she half expected David to come storming after. Tears were streaming, but Kim would say no more, dare not. She opened the back door and was out into the alley, her face stained and red.

Chapter 17

Jack strode down Earlham Grove; he was late, and getting later. The leaves on the plane trees were thinning, the setting sun down the end of the road behind him, throwing long shadows along the tarmac. In another month, this time of day would be night.

He passed his house, not going in to change out of his work clothes, knowing if he did, he wouldn't leave. Ten minutes ago, he'd been due to meet Kim outside Forest Gate station. She'd either be waiting or be gone when he got there. Nothing much he could do about it.

The scene with Maria had left him empty. A stick in the mud was her description. Yes, he was a stick, unadventurous, boring. He should never have gone to see Maria. What did he expect from her? Maybe Kim would still be there. She'd be company, they could talk of this and that. He didn't know what he'd do if she had already gone.

His phone rang as he walked. He looked at the screen. Alison. He almost turned the phone off, not wanting to be bothered, but thought he was probably in her good books. He'd done her repair, a century ago.

'Hello, Alison.'

'Thank you, Jack. I don't thank you that often, but I am so grateful,' she said. 'I didn't know what I was going to do this morning, water pouring through the kitchen ceiling... Luckily, you were just up the road. Thank you. What do I owe you?'

'Forget it,' he said automatically. Money had no meaning.

'No, no, you can't do that. You came. I needed you. If it hadn't been you, I would have had to pay emergency rates to a plumber. How much?'

He lacked the energy to stand his ground. 'Call it a hundred,' he said.

'You sure?'

'You've subbed me often enough. I was going to let you have this one on the house...'

'I'll give you one hundred and twenty,' she said. 'Mia told me there was a mouse stuck in the overflow. And you rescued the beast.' She laughed. 'You always were a softy.'

'The little thing didn't do me any harm,' he said, smiling in spite of himself at the memory of the animal he'd held up by the tail.

'It certainly did me a lot. Not intentionally, mind you. What about the kitchen ceiling? It's bulging.'

'It needs to come down,' he said. 'The middle area at least. Then give the joists a week or two to dry out, and replace the plasterboard and redecorate.'

He was in professional mode. Fine. She was thanking him, listening to him, paying him. She'd got him off forlorn lover mode. Thank you, Alison, he almost said. He noted he'd slowed his pace as he talked. What was another minute?

'Will you do the ceiling, Jack?'

'I could take the plaster down tomorrow,' he said. 'That won't take long. Just be messy. Then we leave it for a couple of weeks to dry out.'

'Do me an estimate, will you? I know you'll be reasonable.'

He stifled a chuckle. He wouldn't dare be otherwise.

'I'll leave it on the kitchen table,' he said.

'Thanks. Is Mia alright? She seems a bit subdued.'

'School, I'm sure.' So she hadn't told Alison about Chitra's visit. Good.

'I suppose so. Teenage stuff. Anyway, thanks again. And so tidy. I'll give you a reference any day of the week.'

They ended the call with a little banter as Jack turned off Earlham Grove into the high street. The first street lights had come on. There was an incline, hardly a hill, from the corner of Earlham Grove up to Forest Gate station, past the Co-op supermarket. He looked out for Kim as he approached but couldn't see her. He glanced at his watch; seventeen minutes late. He hardly knew her. How long would she wait?

She wasn't outside the station. He looked inside. The ticket office had closed. The vestibule wasn't large, leading on to the platforms. Not there either. He went back outside and looked up and down the street. It was late rush hour and quite busy, but no sign of her. Jack was aware of his overalls. This wasn't how you dressed for a date. Then again, it was very likely there wouldn't be a date.

What would he say to her tomorrow? Ages away. He'd find some words sometime.

A train had come in, and commuters poured out of the station. He stayed out of the melee, pulling back against the wall. Amazing how many people can pack on a train, and how many of them alighted at Forest Gate. He looked at his watch again. Twenty minutes late. He should have taken her phone number.

A car hooted and his name was called, causing him to look up. There was Bob, halted at the traffic lights in his van, a pair of long ladders along the top.

'I see you're working late, Jack,' he called.

A reference to his overalls.

'At the cemetery.' He pointed in the direction.

'Don't dig up too many bodies.' Then the lights changed and Bob concentrated. 'Must get together soon. See you, mate.'

'Bye, Bob.'

And his friend was away. A good pal. Bob passed on work to Jack from time to time. Jack used to see more of him in his drinking days. Bob was one of those who couldn't go out without having a drink, while Jack avoided pubs, and drinkers too for that matter.

Twenty-five minutes. Kim had come and gone for sure. He couldn't blame her. It was his fault entirely. Normally he was on time, but today Maria had nullified him. What to do now? He could do some shopping at the Co-op. Alison had lifted him and seeing Bob reminded him he was human. Pity he'd blown his date. But it happened. Quite a clear night. He could buy a snack or two at the Co-op, go home and get his telescope and drive to Wanstead Flats. He wouldn't bother to change.

'I am so sorry, Jack.'

She was there, flustered, breathless. She looked as if she'd been crying.

'The meeting went on for ages,' she said. 'On and on. All the ranting and raving. I didn't have your phone number. Thank you oh so much for waiting. I thought you'd be gone.'

'I was a bit late myself,' he said. She hadn't mentioned his overalls, so he wouldn't. 'Where's this house?'

She put her arm in his. 'Not far. I was sure you'd given up on me. Thanks for sticking around. I'm not usually like this, but things got on top of me.'

Chapter 18

As they walked, the streetlights came on. They went back up Jack's road. He considered suggesting he drop into his house and get changed, but rejected it. He would need to shower, should have a shave, and so would be a good twenty minutes, whereas they were on the move and she didn't seem to mind his clothes. In fact, she couldn't stop talking, though she hung onto his arm securely.

'The meeting was terrible, terrible,' she said pulling at his arm. 'I didn't realise what they were up to. It started off all right. Okaying the last minutes and matters arising. All very formal and tedious. Then my nomination for the board came up. I said a bit about myself, the shares I had inherited, and how I'd known the cemetery almost as long as I can remember.' She stopped, a little self conscious. 'Oh, you know the kind of guff. Everyone was smiling. They either knew me or knew of me. You know how these things go.'

He didn't but he let her go on.

'There was a treasurer's report. Utterly mind-numbing, columns and columns of figures, comparing what was spent with the budget... There, I'm boring you already, well it was lots worse sitting there. I thought, is it going to go on like this?' She took a deep breath and found his hand and held it. 'I didn't see it coming. David began attacking the Chair, his brother, you know Saul. Mum joined in, then Ruth and a couple of others. David proposed a vote of no confidence. That was argued over for ten minutes. Saul saying over and over it should be on the agenda and his wife Sarah would then have a proxy vote. But he lost that and there was to be the vote, then Mr Green called for a secret ballot. More argument. I wanted a secret ballot, but I don't suppose it would have helped me, there were only eight of us there altogether, easy enough to work out who voted for what. The proposal for a secret ballot was lost. David repeated his proposal of no confidence in the Chair, Mum seconded it. Discussion, more discussion, shouting, insults. They were going back ten, twenty years. I couldn't believe the animosity. Then the vote, a hands up thing. It was four votes for the motion and four votes against. Saul informed us he had a casting vote as Chair in the event of a tie, which means really he had two votes. More argument and shouting. But he'd have won even if it had been a dead heat, as the proposal wasn't passed.'

She stopped walking, causing him to stop too. 'Oh, Jack. It was dreadful. Everyone was yelling. The meeting was abandoned and Mum, David and Ruth all had a go at me.'

'Why you?'

'Because I voted for Saul.'

'Why?'

'Because they were all screaming at him and it didn't seem right.'

'You could have...' he searched for the word, 'what do they call it, abstained,' remembering the term from union meetings.

'I could have. Maybe should have, then Mum wouldn't have kicked me out.' She squeezed his hand. 'I'm homeless.'

'So where are you going to sleep tonight?'

'I thought I'd sleep on your sofa.'

He chuckled. He wasn't averse to that.

'You've got this house though,' he said. 'What's that about?'

'I only found out about it a week ago. My husband, soon to be ex, hooray hooray, has had almost everything taken away, proceeds of crime they call it, and tax evasion. But a solicitor, a nice chap, phoned me about the house. Did I know it was in my name? I didn't. I must've signed something about four years ago. Totally forgot, some fiddle of Brad's. Anyway, the solicitor sent me the papers and a key. I got them yesterday at the stall, motorbike delivery. So now I'm going to see the place. Could be a wreck, could be a mansion.'

'I doubt that. Not round here.'

'I've seen some nice places. Hardly mansions, I agree. We turn here. Atherton Road. Number 21.'

'New leisure centre at the end,' he said. 'That'll keep you fit, have a swim every morning.'

'I've plenty of time for it now,' she said. 'Not only homeless, I'm unemployed too. This is it.'

They stopped at a two-storey house.

'I don't understand,' she went on, peering at the house, face screwed in puzzlement. 'I'm sure it's 21. But this house is occupied. The solicitor told me it was empty.'

'Definitely occupied,' said Jack.

The brickwork was sound, the windows painted.

'It's in good repair,' he said. 'New drainpipes and guttering.'

'But it's being lived in,' she said.

Light was showing through the front curtains which were closed. A light was on in the hall. The small front garden was neat, the grass cut short, late roses on the bushes.

'Squatters?' he said.

'Only one way to find out.'

She headed up the path, Jack followed. There was a single bell. She rang it.

'This is a complication,' she said, taking a deep breath. 'I was going to sell the place...'

'Not move in?'

'I've other plans. Tell you later. Someone's coming.'

A silhouette was showing in the glass of the door. The door opened. A man stood there, completely bald, tall and broad, in an open necked shirt. Jack knew him immediately.

'Keith!' exclaimed Kim. 'What are you doing here?'

'It's my house,' he said.

'It's mine,' she declared. 'I have the deeds.'

He smiled at her. 'And I'm here.'

Jack was examining the hallway. It was well painted in orange and red, there was a row of coat hooks with neat coats and hats, under them a small child's bicycle with stabilisers. On the stairs was new carpet. At the back, a door was open to a kitchen where he could just make out units in dark wood.

'How long have you been living here?' she said.

'Some time,' he said, hands on hips.

'And paying no rent.'

He shrugged. 'My brother owns the place. He says I can stay as long as I like.'

'I own it,' she insisted. 'You are squatting, Keith. I shall serve you eviction papers.'

Keith grabbed her by the throat, lifting her off her feet. 'You do, and you'll be dead.'

Jack thrust him in the chest with both hands. 'Take your hands off her.'

Keith dropped Kim and swung a punch at Jack. He pulled away just in time, the blow inches from his face. Kim drew Jack back, out of Keith's sweep, as a young woman came out of the kitchen in an apron and kitchen gloves.

'What's going on here?' she said.

'These people think they own this place,' exclaimed Keith. 'And I'm making it clear they don't.' He waved a fierce finger at Kim. 'You want to survive, you forget this house.' The young woman in the apron put a hand on his shoulder.

'It's our house,' she said.

Keith gave a smile of satisfaction as he slammed the door on his visitors.

Jack and Kim remained on the path for half a minute, as if the door might re-open and they be invited in.

'He's stolen my house,' she exclaimed, her face white with rage.

Jack put a hand under her elbow. 'Let's get a coffee. The Atherton coffee bar will be open. Talk about it there.'

A few minutes later they were at a small table, a coffee each, against the glass of the long window overlooking the Romford Road.

Jack said, 'He's been there, I'd say, 18 months or more. Settled in. The hall is well decorated, walls, doors and ceiling. Good electrics, new carpet on the stairs. What I could see of the kitchen had expensive fittings...'

'It's mine,' she said with finality.

'You must go to the police,' he said. 'He threatened you.'

'I need a lawyer.' She took a deep breath. 'That was most unexpected. Just as well I'm unemployed, I'm going to be busy tomorrow.' She stopped, her face twisted. 'Sorry, Jack, I'm not in the mood to go out for dinner.'

'Let's go to the cop shop.'

Chapter 19

Nora had put out two pizzas and opened a bottle of wine. She, Ruth and David were in her sitting room eating and drinking. The room was sparse and tidy, with new furniture. There was a large print by Jack Vettriano on the wall, a man and a woman dancing on the beach with the butler holding an umbrella over their heads. Nora liked the mystery of the composition, everyone knowing their part whatever the story might be.

She kept the room neat, not allowing clutter on the surfaces, but only selected objects. Though she never felt she had it quite right. Were her tortoises common? She thought of changing to cats, or maybe pigs, but a woman she hated collected pigs and wanted to sell them. But she could sell the tortoises on eBay. Buy pigs.

Or rhinos. Weren't they related?

There was a large flat screen TV, and shelving units with books on early and mid twentieth century fashion along with a line of ceramic tortoises in various styles and sizes. The hundreds of others were kept in the spare room, competing with the racks of vintage clothing. She'd lost storage space when Kim came back. Now she'd given Kim her marching orders, she could have another stock room.

Space, always more space. She must enquire about industrial units. But there was the time and energy expended. No money in it, but you couldn't just look at one place, you had to see three or four before committing yourself. So much effort to risk hard earned money.

She shouldn't have invited David and Ruth back. Well, they'd invited themselves, she lived closest. Nora'd wanted to sort herself out this evening for the Hackney market tomorrow. How long were they going to stay? They seemed settled, and were going through the pizza. Probably a mistake offering wine, they'd only stay longer, but it was quicker to serve than coffee.

She had been in such a temper today. It had taken her over. Did she really want to kick Kim out? Yes and no. Better not to have someone to yell at, but Kim was company. Did she really want to drive her daughter away? She was no spring chicken. Her husband gone, now Kim. She would die alone, she knew it. With no one to blame but herself.

Ruth and David were seated in opposite armchairs, Nora lounged on the sofa between them.

'Any idea where she's staying?' said Ruth.

'No, I don't. A hotel, I suppose. She's got some money.' Nora took a slice of pizza, anxiety increased her appetite. 'Help yourselves, please. Don't let me eat it all.'

'How could you get it so wrong?' retorted David.

'I didn't expect it,' said Nora, throwing her hands up. 'She gave no signs. I don't know what to say to you. I'm sorry. I should have known, but I didn't. I don't know what to say.'

'You don't know much about your daughter, you're telling us,' David exclaimed, 'yet you thought she was the right person to go on the board.'

'Stop attacking me, David. I can't cope. This is doing my head in. Don't go on about the meeting. I've kicked her out. Sorry. I misled you. I thought she'd have some loyalty...' She threw up her hands. 'Totally misplaced.'

'We gather that,' said David, taking a sip of wine. 'We voted her in, on your advice.' He put his hand up to stop another Nora tirade. 'Don't apologise any more, it gets us nowhere. We need an assured majority if we are to carry through the housing deal.'

'How much did he pay her?' mused Ruth.

'You think Saul bribed her?' exclaimed Nora.

'Why else would she side with him?'

'I agree,' said David. 'Saul got in first. We listened to you, Nora. Big mistake.'

'I'm sorry.'

'If I hear that again, I'll throw this pizza at you.'

Ruth and Nora sat back, silenced. No one spoke, concentrating on food and drink. And personal safety.

'We have a clear choice,' said David at last.

'Which is?' said Nora, eating her pizza untidily with her hands, as it crumbled into pieces.

'We either buy her off. Or we kill her.' He chortled.

'Is this what burning bodies all day does to you?' said Ruth.

'We all die, Ruth. The only uncertainty is the date. They come down in the lift, we fill out the sheets. We put them in the oven. One lot of ash looks exactly the same as any other.' He put down his glass. 'I mustn't drink any more of this. I'm driving.' He rubbed his chin. 'I still have a soft spot for Kim. But there is a limit.'

'We voted her in,' exclaimed Nora. 'I'm…' She stopped herself from another apology. 'How dare my own daughter do this! I can't believe it. I took her back in when she had nowhere to go, much against my better judgement, and look how she treats me!'

'I think they call it the Electra Complex,' said Ruth. 'Don't they? Greek mythology. She blames you for driving her father away.'

'She hated the bastard!' retorted Nora. 'The one thing we have in common is hatred of Mick.'

'Let's get back to what happened today,' said David brusquely. 'We aimed to depose Saul. And we failed. That's where we are. Now what?'

'Don't forget Sarah in all this,' said Ruth. 'Whatever we think of Saul, he's taken good care of her since the accident.'

David waved his hands dismissively. 'Oh, Sarah will be all right whatever happens. She's got her trust fund.'

'A nurse is not the same as a husband,' said Ruth.

'You can fire a nurse,' said Nora. 'Husbands are more trouble.'

David hit the table with his fist. Glasses and plates jumped. 'Shut up! Can we not stick to the subject for one minute?'

Nora and Ruth looked at each other. Nora rolled her eyes; her brother again.

'If it's a question of money,' said David, thinking aloud, 'we could offer Kim, say, twenty thou...'

'That much!' exclaimed Ruth.

'Murder is cheaper, if you'd rather,' said David. 'But it happens to be illegal.'

'Sometimes you surprise me, David,' said Ruth. 'There must be another way. We can't give Kim a king's ransom for doing nothing.'

'It's the way of the world.'

'I wouldn't trust her anyway,' said Ruth. 'Not after this afternoon.'

'Are you suggesting murder then?'

'Stop it,' yelled Nora. 'You're talking about my daughter. I will not have it. She's my flesh and blood. Yours too. Uncle and aunty. She's not a kitten to be thrown in the pond in a sack.'

'Quite right,' said Ruth. 'Let's be realistic. She is family. None of this talk of killing. I am coming round to your other suggestion.' She sighed. 'It has to be money. Saul bought her, we can buy her back.'

'I'd rather enjoy outbidding Saul,' said David.

'She's not poor,' said Nora. 'She's got her cemetery shares, and held on to some money out of the wreck of her marriage. That is, I think she did. And then yesterday, she got a house. I don't know how, something the law didn't claw back. On Atherton Road. Came out of the blue. I saw the letter on the kitchen table. I couldn't believe it. She does absolutely nothing – and it comes to her. Like manna from heaven. Me? I started work at sixteen. I've never stopped slaving away, while money rains down on her.'

'Lucky girl,' said David. He pushed the pizza away. 'We have to talk to her.'

'I don't know where she is.'

'She'll turn up. Which of us is she more likely to listen to?'

Chapter 20

Jack and Kim had gone to Jack's place and phoned for a Chinese takeaway. While waiting for their meal to arrive, Jack had a shower, pleased to get out of his overalls and wash off the dirt of work. He changed the plaster on the back of his hand, and put on a clean T-shirt and jeans just before their meal arrived. He was abashed to see that she'd been tidying the sitting room, and relieved she didn't get as far as the kitchen which had the detritus of the last two days.

The *Special Set Dinner for Two* from Moon House was placed on the table in the metal trays the selection came in. Jack put a spoon in each for serving, and washed two plates without disturbing the heap in the sink. He ate hungrily, while Kim put a little on her plate which she barely touched. Just as well they hadn't gone to a restaurant, he thought. At least he'd have the leftovers for tomorrow.

'Don't you like it?' he said.

'I don't feel like eating,' she said. 'I keep thinking of Keith in my house.'

'The cops said they'll go and see him,' he said. 'That'll make him think twice.'

She shrugged. 'The desk sergeant didn't seem that interested,' said Kim. 'He'd rather I was murdered. Much more exciting than a common or garden threat.'

'They'll warn Keith,' insisted Jack. 'They've got our statements on record.'

'That's nice to know,' she said with a shudder and pushed aside her plate. 'Sorry. It's not the food. It's me.'

Not the greatest of first dates, thought Jack. We skip the restaurant, get a takeaway and she doesn't want to eat any.

He thought of putting some music on but she looked so morose. This was going to be one of those evenings. He was fed up with discussing Keith. He'd been the only topic in the café, on the way to the police station, giving the statement, and since. Keith had taken over their evening. He might as well have been sitting at the table.

Now she was here, he was stuck with her for the night. She had nowhere else to go. But all she could think of was Keith and the house. Then again, he wasn't the one threatened, but he had hoped for some romance.

Fat chance.

But he was hungry even if she wasn't, having worked hard on top of being soaked. It was five hours since he'd last eaten. Ages ago at Alison's, before he'd met Maria and she'd made her offer of an open relationship. Freedom, sauced with jealousy. She'd hardly be jealous of what was going on here.

'You could make a will,' he said, out of desperation to say something.

'Make it out to you, you mean, just in case I pop off in the next few days.'

Not the brightest thing for him to say. He knew it as soon as the words were coming out. But he couldn't sit here in silence. He spooned out some rice.

'This is special fried rice,' he said. 'Doesn't seem special to me. Just ordinary fried rice with a few peas and bits of chicken in. It's not bad though. You could try some.'

'I'm awful company,' she said with a sigh. 'They've all had a go at me. Uncle David, Mum, Auntie Ruth. When Mum kicked me out, I thought at least I've got a house – but I haven't. That lowlife's snatched it.'

Jack added the beef and green peppers in bean sauce to the heap of rice on his plate. It reminded him of a concrete mix and the work he'd done today. He turned it over with a fork, could never manage chopsticks, too fussy and fiddly.

'If Keith murders me sharpish,' she said, 'I'll still be married, Brad will be a sad widower and inherit the house.'

Jack put down his fork. 'I know what I said before sounded crazy. But maybe not. You should make a will. Leave it to someone who would definitely evict Keith.'

'How would that help?'

'Let's suppose he kills you.' He held out a hand to fend off her reaction. 'I'm not wishing it on you, just supposing the worst.'

'OK,' she said. 'I'm dead. Now what?'

'There's a will. And Brad is not the beneficiary.'

'So Keith will have to leave,' she exclaimed, catching up. 'So there's no point killing me, if all that happens is the house is left to someone who will evict him.'

'Got it. He'd risk a life sentence for nothing.' He stopped as a thought intervened, 'Hang about. I've got a will form. A basic one. I downloaded it from the internet. Just in case I fall off a rooftop, I want to leave everything to my daughter. But I haven't got round to filling it in.'

Jack rose and went to the sideboard.

'Somewhere amongst this lot. My filing system.'

The surface was a shambles of papers, books, magazines, a pair of scissors, a screwdriver, a box of screws and miscellaneous oddments which obviously Kim had left in place in her tidy up, not wanting to mess up his system.

'Here it is,' he exclaimed, impressed he had found it. 'I've got three copies of it. It's only a page.' He handed the papers to her. 'Take a look.'

'There's nothing much to it,' she said, perusing it. 'Full name, date of birth. Got a pen?' He handed her one and she filled in the spaces with a rapid scrawl. 'Address. What do I put down for that? Mum's place. I've still got my stuff there.' She wrote the address. 'Now who do I leave all my worldly worth to?' She contemplated the possibilities, sucking the end of the pen. 'I'm not giving my mum a thing. And as she won't be leaving me anything, we are quits.'

'Someone who will definitely evict,' said Jack. 'An organisation.'

'Canning Town Cattery!' she exclaimed laughing. 'That would really rattle Mum. She hates cats.' Then shook her head. 'That's no good. Just a couple of old women run it. Keith could easily scare them off.'

'You need a big outfit. Lots of workers and committees.'

'Right. Battersea Dogs & Cats Home. They're a huge charity, with enough company lawyers to fill a football ground.' She filled in the spaces, then signed the will. 'That's satisfying. If Keith cuts my throat and gets away with it, he will be out on the streets with that pretty wife of his.' She held out the pen to him. 'Witness it and date it.'

Jack took the form from her. Her writing was just about readable. It would do. He signed on the dotted line, and added the date.

'So what do I do with it?' she said, folding the will in half.

'Fill in the other two. Then send him a copy so he can see it would be a waste of time bumping you off. Send another to your lawyer...' He spooned out more fried rice. 'I'm eating all this, you know.'

'Good. Then it won't go to waste.' She stood up. 'You've cheered me up, Jack. I'll make us a cup of tea.'

'I'll do it,' he said hurriedly, not wanting her to go into the kitchen.

'You finish eating,' she said, a hand on his shoulder, stopping him rising. 'You're working tomorrow; I'm a lady of leisure.'

'You've got to see a solicitor,' he said. 'To hold the will, to serve notice on Keith. And you need to find somewhere to live.'

'Just as I was cheering up, you've reminded me. Flat hunting is such tedium. Though I could take one of those overpriced apartments in Stratford. Just for a few months. I'm planning to start a coffee shop. I wasn't in a rush, but I am now. If I could find a suitable shop with a flat over it... Somewhere to live and work.' She stopped with a sigh. 'I'm too used to being looked after. That's my trouble. It becomes debilitating after a couple of years. I should thank them all at the meeting today, for giving me a good kicking. And all I did was put my hand in the air.'

She went into the kitchen. He waited for her to yell at the mess, but she didn't. It was only when he had someone over that he tidied up. Mostly for Mia, when she was here. Or sometimes Mia did it for him. Today, he'd slotted in quarter of an hour to clear up but the meeting with Maria had blown his timetable. He really should do the chores as he went along, but it seemed such a waste of energy. The mess simply built up again. He could see himself as a pensioner existing in a cave of bottles, cans and takeaway boxes, his living space getting smaller by the day. Until it swallowed him up.

When was the last time he'd washed the kitchen floor? He tried to recall. Yes, Mia had done it, New Year's Day. Begin the New Year with a clean floor, she'd said. So, OK, it was his turn. Kitchen floor. Every nine months, whether it needs it or not.

Kim came out of the kitchen.

'You haven't got a dishwasher,' she said.

'Not a priority.'

She put her arms over his shoulders and kissed him on the back of the neck.

'I'm going to add a codicil to my will, and leave you a few hundred to buy one.'

Chapter 21

'Who's that?'

'This is Mia.'

'How did you get my number, Mia?'

'With a lot of difficulty. I've been phoning around, been on Facebook and the rest of them. Anita gave me it.'

'So what do you want?'

'You know what I want, Chitra.'

'Do I?'

'Yes. You were round my house thieving. My dad told me.'

'I didn't know it was your house. Your dad's that builder? He's alright. I thought he was going to call the cops. But he didn't.'

'He gave you a tenner and let you take some food.'

'He did. Nice guy. I never expected it.'

'Enough about my dad. You've got my bracelet.'

'Ah! That's what this is about.'

'It is. A silver chain with tiny teddy bears hanging from it.'

'Bit babyish, isn't it?'

'So why you keeping it?'

'I didn't know I had it. I thought I gave everything back to your dad. It was only when I left that I found it in my pocket.'

'I want it back.'

'Fine. Come and get it.'

'It's late.'

'Don't then.'

'Where are you?'

'I'll be outside Forest Gate Cemetery in ten minutes.'

'I'll be there.'

Jack and Kim were arm in arm, walking up Earlham Grove. It was past eleven o'clock, the night sky overcast. The street lights were too bright to allow stars to show, even if there were any, though the moon was visible as an amorphous glow in the clouds. The wind was chilly. Jack had loaned Kim a woolly hat and he wore one himself. The Victorian houses had their curtains drawn, shutting away the life inside. Way down the street a man was walking with a dog, the only person in sight.

'What's with you and your mother?' he said.

'We argue all the time,' she said. 'She treats me like a ten year old.'

'You said she kicked you out.'

She shrugged. 'Yeh. I expect I could go back, grovel, but I don't want to. It's her place and doesn't she let me know it. She keeps telling me how to live my life, how she started work at sixteen. And no one owes anyone a living. Blah blah blah.'

'I'm sure that's exhausting.'

'She works non-stop. Makes me feel guilty watching TV in the evenings. But she went bankrupt five years ago. There she was, piling up properties, her ambition to be a multi millionaire. She had about twenty houses, but it wasn't enough for her to be rich. Too many people with more. Including me. Ha ha. So she borrowed, bought more houses, got so overstretched that it all came a-tumble down in the recession. She was caught, owing money everywhere, in negative equity. The banks hammered on the door for their pound of flesh. And that was the end of that. She lost the lot. Even the house she was living in.'

'She seems to have bounced back.'

'She was devastated. Heartbroken. All those millions lost. And I mean millions. But six months later, like the busy spider she is, she's off again, spinning her web. Starting with the flower stall, and now she has a couple of other stalls selling vintage clothing in markets in Hackney and Camden. She never stops running around, buying, selling. I don't know how much she's got put by now. Not enough, never enough. It's sad. If she'd been less greedy, settled for say a dozen houses, she'd be very comfortable, but no – she wants to join the exclusive club on the Riviera. Or bust.'

'I can see she'd be difficult to live with.'

'She's OK in small doses. Visits. Not living and working for her. Stuff her flower stall! She'll have to take someone on. And I don't envy them one bit.'

Jack mused on his own mother as Kim spoke. Small doses was about right. At least he'd made contact again. He mostly went to see her along with Mia. Conversation was easier then. Though she had the TV on all the time. At least it was something to talk about beyond her church and rules on how life should be lived.

They stopped outside the contested house. The light was on in the curtained front room. Keith and his wife were still up. Sweet domesticity. A neat house, in good repair, thought Jack. With a violent man living there. Kim left him and ran up the path. She pushed an envelope through the letterbox. And then hurried back.

'Let's get away,' she said, putting her arm in his. 'In case he heard it drop and comes out.'

They headed back the way they'd come.

Chapter 23

Mia could just hear the TV from her mother's bedroom as she crept down the stairs to the hallway. There, she removed her jacket from the hallway hooks, clutching it in her arms as she opened the front door, and then closing the door as quietly as she could. And she was away, putting on her jacket, doing up her zip, getting the woolly hat from the pocket, adjusting it as she walked swiftly along the pavement. She'd grabbed the clothes she wore for going out with her dad on stargazing nights. In her pocket were the fingerless gloves she used to work the telescope on cold nights.

A car went by, but she was the only walker on the silent street, keeping close to the hedges, nervous at being on her own, out so late. It was barely five minutes' walk to the cemetery, though why meet there she couldn't fathom. Not that she intended staying long; get the bracelet and head back home. Her mother wouldn't even know that she'd gone.

A man came out of a side road, crossed to her side and walked towards her, tall and hidden in a hood. She crossed over the road to get clear of him. As the figure passed, he glanced over, perhaps no more than curiosity, but how can you know?

She'd left her phone at home. Why would she need it? Who would she phone so late? But suppose Chitra wasn't there? Too late for such thoughts. She'd better be there and have the bracelet. This could be a waste of time, if so Mia would harry her to the grave. It was a matter of pride. Chitra had called it babyish. So what? She loved that little bracelet.

There she was, ahead, by the cemetery gate. She must be cold, no hat, no coat, striding up and down flapping her arms.

'Took your time,' said Chitra.

'No, I didn't. I left almost immediately. Have you got it?'

'It's in my house,' said Chitra.

'Where's that?'

Without replying Chitra went to the cemetery gate. She took out a key from her pocket and opened the gate.

'Where did you get a key?'

Chitra shrugged. 'They have too many. Easy to get one.' She was holding the gate slightly open. 'Get in quick.'

'There's no houses in there.'

'Mine is.' Adding impatiently, 'Come on. I don't want to be seen holding the gate open.'

Mia went in, and Chitra locked up after her.

'Keep to the shadows,' said Chitra, 'then no one'll see us.'

'I don't like it here. It's scary. All the graves, all the skeletons.'

'They're dead,' said Chitra. 'Just worry about the living.' She took her arm. 'You're OK with me. No bogies will get you.'

Once away from the gate, they were in almost complete darkness. Trees were just visible, black against a deep purple sky. They went by the empty flower stall, the plants locked away. Up ahead was the stark steeple of the crematorium. A train clattered by on the nearby track, the sound falling away as it passed, as if it were being slowly turned off like a gas tap.

'This is spooky. Where's your house? I don't know how you can come in here so late.'

'This is safe,' said Chitra. 'Believe me.' She stopped. 'We're here.'

She was by a mausoleum, a stone edifice with gothic angles at the top of its walls, as high as a tall man. There was a low door in the front wall which Chitra pushed open.

'I'm not going in there,' exclaimed Mia.

'Wait a minute then.' She went inside, leaving the door ajar.

'What are you doing in there?' hissed Mia.

'Lighting a candle. And you don't have to whisper. No one can hear us. Unless you believe in ghosts.'

Though she might plead otherwise, Mia's trembling body most surely did. In daylight she'd boldly say ghosts are just imagination. In a cemetery, past midnight, at the open door of a mausoleum, she'd make no such claim, lest she offend the dark forces.

'You can come in now.'

Cautiously, Mia entered, breathing rapidly. The low-ceilinged space was lit by a fat, square candle on a waist-high shelf, throwing flickering shadows on the walls.

'Close the door.'

Mia did so reluctantly.

The floor was stone slabs, clear to the walls. At the far end in the centre was an alcove with two Grecian-type urns on small shelves, one above the other. On both side walls were two wide shelves, the length of the wall. There were three coffins on them, one of the lower shelves was vacant.

'There's bodies there!' exclaimed Mia, indicating the coffins as she backed off to the door. 'We shouldn't be here.'

'Bones, just bones,' said Chitra. 'They can't hurt you.'

She went to a coffin on a lower shelf and lifted the lid. Mia covered her face in fear of what might leap out. Opening her eyes a few seconds later, she saw Chitra holding a cushion which she placed regally on the floor.

'Be my guest.'

Mia sank to the floor, her legs hollow. 'That coffin...' she began, pointing to the one Chitra had opened.

'I keep my stuff in it,' said Chitra, sitting down cross-legged. 'Sleeping bag, clothes, whatever. I don't want to leave anything on the floor when I leave each day, in case someone comes in. Though it's unlikely anyone will, but you never know. It did have a body in, bones actually, scraps of cloth. I moved it all to the top coffin.'

'You moved the bones?' Mia shivered, imagining a jangly skeleton with a grinning skull, remnants of clothing crawling with beetles. 'It's disrespectful,' she added. 'It's grave robbing.'

'I said a prayer,' said Chitra. 'I apologised and told her, I think it's a her, why I needed the coffin.' She shrugged. 'She was buried a long time ago. From the inscription on the outside wall, the last one was put here in 1896.'

'I bet you're the first in here since.'

'I found the key in their keybox. In the office.' She gave a superior sniff. 'They won't even know it's gone.'

'It's very clean here,' said Mia looking about her.

'It wasn't when I first came. But I borrowed a pan and brush from the office...'

'Stole, you mean.'

Chitra shrugged. 'I might give it back. I gave back the mop and bucket after I washed the floor. Got rid of all the dust and spiders.'

'You are brave.'

'I'm safe in here,' she said and smiled. 'You're my first guest, Mia. Would you like some chocolate?'

Chapter 24

Kim put down her cup. She and Jack were in bed, clothes discarded on the floor as if blown there by a hurricane. They were half under the duvet, bodies touching at hips and legs. The Pastorale was playing on the bedside CD player.

'I'm surprised at your music, Jack.'

'Don't you like it?'

'I do. But you'd never hear Beethoven on building sites.'

He chuckled and squeezed her hand. 'Mia brought it over. She was studying it in school for music. She explained it to me. I was quite knocked out. I thought I hated classical music. Posh people in dinner jackets.'

'Where's yours?' She scratched his chest.

He closed his eyes as she massaged.

'This first movement, don't know why they call them movements,' he said, 'is all about being in the countryside. Sunshine, fields, forest. It ends with a cuckoo, two calls. I always listen out for them. Then there's a stream and a peasant dance. That's broken up by a storm. I can see everyone running for shelter. And then the sun comes out and it's country sounds, back to the picnic and dancing.' He brought her hand to his lips, kissing the knuckle. 'I hardly learnt a thing at school, let alone classical music. Like a prison camp. I couldn't wait to get out.' He laughed at a memory. 'Alison told me, in the middle of a spat, that I was a pig ignorant builder.'

'You know about astronomy,' said Kim in his defence. 'I saw magazines and a telescope in the sitting room.'

'I know a little.'

'Bet she doesn't know any.'

She kissed the inside of his arm, following up to his shoulder.

'I was a pig to her though,' he said as she climbed onto him. 'Pig to the world. Ignorant with it.' He massaged her back. 'Until I started looking at the stars. The patterns in the sky. I learnt about the universe, some science, how nothing stays the same. And now Mia tells me stuff she's learning, I read her text books sometimes. I expect in a year or two they'll be a bit much.' He stopped, his hands in the small of her back. 'You know what I'd like to learn?'

'Tell me.'

'Architecture. I've worked in lots of buildings. I'm fascinated how they stay up, or fall down. All decorative, fancy bits. The Victorians, they went in for pillars and scrolls and arches. But then you have the sixties boxes, no extras, done on the cheap. I'd like to know more about Tudor houses, all wood and wattle. I read that in Mia's history book, looking at the pictures. I like the way their houses are wonky. I'm not anti modern stuff, steel and glass high rise. I watch the towers going up in Stratford, pillars on the floors going through like cake stands, layer on layer, up and up.' He laughed as she tickled a hand down his thigh. 'That's nice.'

'I like learning about your education.'

'It was being married to a teacher that woke me up. She'd take me round museums and ramble on. I was dead bored to start with. Another museum! I'll see you in the café, I'd say. But I picked up scraps, here and there, and began to get interested.'

'I think there's a university professor in you, fighting to get out.' She tweaked his nose. 'Though I prefer you in overalls.'

They sank into an embrace. Jack had a fleeting thought of Maria, almost hoping she was watching them, as they rolled on the mattress.

His phone rang.

'What the hell!'

They broke apart.

'Better answer it,' she said. 'You never know.'

He picked up the phone with a sigh. Alison. It'd better be important.

'What is it?' he said.

'Mia's missing. I went in her bedroom. And she wasn't there. Her bed hasn't been slept in.'

'Have you tried phoning her?'

'She left her phone behind,' she said in annoyance. 'I've called the police. It's one thirty, Jack. She could be anywhere. A thirteen year old girl. Anything could have happened.'

'I'll be right over,' he said. And closed the call.

He turned to Kim. 'Did you get that?'

'I could hear most of it. Mia's gone missing. You'd better go.'

He kissed her on the lips, pressing her against him. She accepted for a few seconds, then thrust him away.

'Off you go.'

He got out of bed, searching the floor for underwear and socks. 'I'll be back soon as I can. Might be nothing. Or a boy. You know, teenagers.'

'I was one once. A million years ago.' She lay back on the pillow, hands under her head. 'A lot of trouble, I can tell you. I must speak to Mum. I give her a hard time. And she isn't altogether wrong. Just most of the time. There's the cuckoo.' She listened to the trill, a finger in the air. 'And again.'

Ten minutes later, Jack was at Alison's. She answered the door in a long paisley dressing-gown, blonde hair draping over her shoulders. Her face was drawn, no make-up. He followed her into the kitchen, where she poured him a coffee.

'I looked at her phone,' she said. 'She'd made a call just after eleven to someone called Chitra.'

'Chitra,' he said. The name bringing him back to the afternoon, to the Asian girl he'd caught stealing. 'She's a school friend,' he added, not wanting to go into details, if he could help it.

'Where does she live?'

'No idea.'

'Why go and see her this time of night? I'd have agreed to a sleepover.'

You might not, thought Jack, wondering if Mia was out stealing with her? Surely not. Except she could be. He took a deep breath.

'You know something I don't,' she said.

He nodded. There was no way out. He was going to have to come clean.

He told her about Chitra being here when he'd come in the afternoon, how he'd emptied her bag of stolen goods, but, in the end, let her go. When he'd finished Alison was silent for half a minute.

'And you weren't going to tell me?' she said at last.

'I've told you now.'

'You told Mia, but you weren't going to tell me. Would you care to explain why?'

'I knew I'd get this from you,' he said. 'You're a head teacher. I knew you'd have me over the coals.'

'She's a burglar, Jack. She went through this house stealing anything she could lay her hands on.'

'Lucky I came, wasn't it?'

Alison ignored him. 'So you let her go. And she's off to another house or two, gathering whatever takes her fancy.'

'And you'd have phoned the cops and social services,' he said. 'Then what? Her stepfather raped her. What sort of place would they take her to, if they didn't send her back home?'

'It's a good job Jack of All Trades was there to make an on-the-spot assessment. Well done, Jack. You've all the appropriate qualifications, I hope.'

'Can we get off this?' he exclaimed, holding his hands up to fend off further attack.

'Mia wouldn't be with her if you'd called the police.'

That was unarguable.

'I thought about it,' he said. 'She's as skinny as a rake. Only a couple of years older than Mia...'

'So you gave her food and a ten pound note.'

'Yep.'

They sat in silence. Jack looked up at the ceiling, stained by a wet patch, bulging in the centre. That was a job he no longer had, once Alison had done with him. Weariness struck him. He'd been wide awake with Kim, an evening that began badly but had blossomed. Just 25 minutes ago he'd been with her, contented, listening to music, alive to the world. Then a phone call, and he was here, being reprimanded.

He said, 'Chitra came in through the back door. She said your latch was useless.'

'A regular little lock picker. There's someone safe on the streets.'

Jack shook his head, a smile escaped him. Alison always had to win.

'I don't know what you think is so funny.'

He started to say something about her, then stopped. It was an old record, played too often. Worn through.

'I'm going to go for a drive around,' he said. 'You never know, I might spot her.'

'With a bag of swag.' She gave a half grin in spite of herself, adding, 'I'd better stay, the cops are due.'

Chapter 25

Mia and Chitra were nibbling chocolate, sharing a 7-Up which they passed between them. Chitra had draped a sleeping bag round herself. Mia kept her outdoor clothes on as it was chilly in the stone room. The candle was half through, a pool of wax around the wick, the flame yellow and smoky, flickering as they spoke throwing their juddering shadows on walls and ceiling.

'I'm getting used to this place,' said Mia, with a slight shiver. 'Sort of. It's like a cave. I've almost forgotten the dead bodies up there. Though you wouldn't catch me here on my own.' She had a thought. 'What do you do about clean clothes?'

'I steal them. Throw dirty stuff away.' Chitra grinned, her eyes lighting up. 'I took a pair of your knickers.'

'How dare you! Give them back.'

'Take them off me. I'm wearing them now.'

'Is nothing safe with you?'

'I didn't know it was your house. Not at first anyway. I promise I won't go back. Your dad was good to me. Have some more chocolate.'

She broke off half a dozen squares and handed them to Mia.

'You haven't been here that long,' said Mia as she munched.

'How d'you know?'

'You don't have any warm clothes. So you can't have been here in winter.' She licked round her lips, chocolate in her teeth, then said, 'You can have my jumper.'

'You don't have to. I can get clothes easily enough.'

Mia had already taken her jacket off.

'I've seen you shivering.' She stripped off the blue, red and yellow striped jumper and handed it over. 'Put it on.'

Chitra looked at it, feeling the wool. It was good quality, well knitted and thick. Decision made, she pulled it over her head and put her arms into the sleeves.

'It's cosy,' she said. 'Thanks. I won't throw it away. Promise.'

'Good to see you warm.' She put her jacket back on. 'You'd better give me the bracelet. I have to get back before Mum wakes up.'

Chitra went to the lower urn at the back of the mausoleum. She put her hand behind it and brought out the bracelet. She handed it to Mia.

'There. Sorry.'

'It's fine,' she said. 'Thank you for showing me your home.'

'Please don't tell anyone.'

'I won't.'

'Promise?'

'I said I won't. Now I must go.'

Chitra rose. 'I'll see you to the gate. No, I'll walk you home.'

'You don't have to.'

'You have to be kind to guests,' she said. 'Especially when they've given you a pair of knickers.'

They laughed. Chitra went to the door and pushed it open.

'Go out, while you can see.'

Mia rose and went to the door. She stepped out, the chill of a night breeze catching her; she half regretted giving up her jumper. She looked back, and saw Chitra blow out the candle. And lost her in the darkness. But in a few seconds, she'd joined her at the entrance.

Chitra closed the door behind them. 'Shall I lock it? Think I'd better, as I'm seeing you home.'

She locked up, then took Mia's arm and they headed for the gate.

'I have to be careful, coming and going,' she said. She stopped in some alarm. 'What's that?'

'There's someone at the gate,' whispered Mia.

They were by the flower stall and could see a couple of figures at the gate, their silhouettes caught in a nearby streetlight. Chitra pulled Mia under the trestle table. They watched as the gate opened.

'They're coming in. Let's back up.'

They inched backwards until they were resting against the wall of the flower shed. Chitra put a finger on Mia's lips.

The gate clanged. Two people were in, walking towards them, their footsteps faint on the tarmac. As they came closer, further from the streetlight, they lost form. Only their movement separated them from the background.

They stopped opposite the flower stall. A light went on in a hand, revealing the two, who had their backs to the girls. A woman in a woolly hat, a man in a trilby, both in short coats. One of them held a phone which was shone on the office door. They heard a jingle of keys and the door opened with a creak. The pair went in, closing the door after them.

Chitra took Mia by the hand. 'We'd better get further back, the inside light's going to go on.'

They rose as the light inside the office went on. Chitra led them behind the shed.

'We're OK here,' she said quietly. The office light was spilling past the sides of the shed. 'Those people, I recognised the woman. She's from the flower stall, I know the man too. Why are they here so late? I always have the cemetery to myself.'

'What are we going to do?' whispered Mia. 'We can't get out the gate without them knowing.'

'We'll have to leave by the back gate. It's a bit of a trek through the cemetery. And then a longer walk home. Sorry.'

'Can't be helped. Please, let's go.'

Chitra took her arm and led her through a maze of gravestones and on to a roadway. Mia had lost all sense of direction, just knowing they were deep in the cemetery. It was so dark, black trees on purple black, no clear direction as far as Mia could discern.

'Don't worry. I know the way,' said Chitra. 'I've done it often enough. But I haven't a key for the back gate. We'll have to climb over.'

Chapter 26

Jack did a tour of Forest Gate. In his van, he stitched up and down the side roads off the high street. There were few people about, and little traffic. If the girls were house-breaking, they could be in any of the houses, going through drawers, taking bits and pieces. He'd never spot them. But would Mia really be doing that? She had pocket money, savings even. Not like Chitra who had only what she stole.

Surely Mia wouldn't join her in burglary. But why had she gone to Chitra so late? Teenagers can be blockheads; he remembered his own years, delighting in breaking rules.

Driving slowly down the wide roads of the Woodgrange estate, he kept an eye out on both sides of the road, so he wouldn't miss them if they were about. The roads were named after royal castles: Windsor, Hampton, Claremont, Osborne, running straight for half a mile. Well lit, with faux gaslights, actually electric, to match the period of the houses. There were no pedestrians on either side of the road.

Chitra must have something that Mia wants, he thought. Something she'd kept back. That was the only way he could explain it. Whatever it was meant a lot to Mia. And she wanted it back desperately. Chitra had said come and get it, to wherever that might be. But why now, in the early hours?

Because Mia was thirteen and impatient.

Think logically, he told himself. Mia wouldn't go far. Not this late. What had Chitra said to him when he'd asked her where she lived? Here and there. Which is another way of saying homeless.

So, say a maximum of ten minutes' walk from Mia's. A homeless girl would have some sort of shelter from the weather. Wanstead Flats was too open, West Ham Park too far. An empty shop perhaps. Under one of the railway arches. Forest Gate cemetery. Too spooky surely, all those graves. Yet perfectly safe, if you are not afraid of vampires. Chitra had struck him as pretty fearless. Would she be staying in the graveyard?

He wouldn't do it himself. Then he reflected, maybe he would've done in his homeless weeks when Alison had thrown him out. If he hadn't been so drunk, and could climb over the fence.

Jack pulled over and turned off the engine. He could hardly keep his eyes open, rubbing them with his fingers. Was there any chance of sleep tonight? He'd drop off at the wheel, if he wasn't careful, and hit something. Where on earth was Mia? He hoped she was with Chitra, doing whatever they were doing. At least the two together were likely to be safe. But a thirteen year old girl, out on the streets this late, on her own. He could only think the worst.

No wonder Alison had had a go at him.

A car was coming towards him. He was dazzled in the headlights, putting up his hands to shield his eyes. As the car came past, he glanced at the driver. Wasn't that Saul Coe from the cemetery? A bit late to be doing accounts.

Jack made a decision. He'd try the cemetery. He had no other ideas. And then go back to Alison's. He could phone her of course, find out if Mia had come home by herself. But then Alison would phone him. Wouldn't she?

Chapter 27

'So what time was it when you found she'd gone?'

The speaker was a young constable in uniform, seated opposite Alison in her kitchen. He was tall, thin, clean shaven, with short brown hair. He was jotting notes as Alison answered, quite slowly which irritated her. Unfairly she knew, but she wanted him, everyone, out there, searching.

'About eleven thirty, I looked in her bedroom,' she said. 'Mia stays up reading sometimes, and I have to take the book away. Or she falls asleep with her headphones on. But she wasn't there.'

'She phoned...' he searched his notes, 'this Chitra about eleven o'clock, we know from Mia's phone. You've tried phoning Chitra yourself?'

'About ten times.' She pushed back her hair. 'Her phone's off. Or out of battery. I don't know. I've no idea where she lives or I'd have been round there.'

The constable perused his notes.

'Are any of your daughter's clothes gone?' he said. 'Or a suitcase? A rucksack?'

'I've looked,' said Alison. 'It did occur to me, though I can't think why she'd run away. She's not unhappy.' She stopped, recalling the first part of the question. 'Difficult to say with clothes, but nothing I've noticed. No suitcase or rucksack gone. But she's left her phone here. If she was going away for whatever reason, she wouldn't leave her phone.'

'Unless she had another one.'

'Oh, now you're really worrying me.'

'Sorry, Mrs Bell. But teenagers can be devious.'

'I think she just popped out, for not very long,' exclaimed Alison. 'And that's why I'm so worried. A thirteen year old girl. Who knows who she's with? They could be holding her against her will. Drugs, sex. I'm afraid to think what could be happening.'

The constable glanced at his phone. 'It's ten past three now. So she's been gone over three hours...'

'At least.'

'You've given me a photo, Mrs Bell. We'll put the information out. And that's about all we can do for the moment. Mostly kids just turn up. In the morning, you must phone round her contacts, go through them all, one at a time. We'll contact the school...'

The front door opened. There were voices. Alison jumped up and immediately ran out to the hallway.

'She's here! She's back! Where on earth have you been, Mia? We've been worried sick.'

Jack was there with a sheepish Mia. He had his arm round her protectively.

'Sorry,' she mumbled into the carpet, sleepy, her face smutty.

'We've got the police here. What a to-do!' Alison ushered Jack and Mia into the kitchen. 'She's here, officer. I am so relieved. Thank you so much for coming, I was so worried...'

The constable stood up. 'And where have you been, young lady?'

'I caught her and Chitra climbing over the cemetery fence,' said Jack.

'And you are, sir?'

'Jack Bell, her father.'

'Thank you.' He put a note in his book, and turned back to Mia. 'What were you doing in the cemetery?'

'It was a dare,' she said weakly. 'Chitra said I was too scared to spend an hour sitting on a gravestone.'

'You're mad!' yelled Alison. 'Absolutely bonkers!'

'And where's Chitra?' said the constable.

'She ran off,' said Jack. 'I couldn't handle two of them. Didn't want to leave Mia.'

The constable nodded and turned back to Mia. 'So you didn't vandalise the cemetery? No graffiti?'

'No,' she shook her head vehemently. 'We were just sitting, talking.'

'If any vandalism is reported,' he said, 'you will be charged. Remember that. It'll go better for you if you admit it now.'

'We didn't do any damage,' said Mia. 'Honest, Dad, honest, Mum.'

The constable turned to Jack and Alison. 'I'll be off, now that she's back safely.' He turned back to Mia. 'It was a stupid thing to do. All sorts of nasty people are out late at night. I've seen more than enough of them. So I'm only too glad you're back safely, young lady.'

'Thank you so much, constable,' said Alison. 'I appreciate your coming. I just want to apologise for my daughter.'

'I'm just glad she's safe, madam.'

Alison saw him out. Jack turned to his daughter who had sat down at the table.

'I must have driven round Forest Gate six times,' he said.

'Sorry.'

'I thought she can't be in the cemetery, she's too sensible. But I looked anyway, in case I was wrong...'

'It was a dare,' she insisted, her head lolled on the table. 'A stupid dare. All my fault. Don't blame Chitra.'

Alison had returned.

'That was so embarrassing,' she exclaimed, sweeping back her hair. 'I was imagining kidnapping, drugs, wild sex parties...'

'Oh Mum!'

'I'm going to get you to bed right away. I want some sleep tonight, I'm totally exhausted.' She turned to Jack. 'I suppose I should thank you for finding her...'

'I was as worried as you were.'

'Thank you, anyway.'

A few minutes later, Jack left. So relieved Mia was safe. Hardly believing she'd be at the cemetery, he'd driven to the back entrance first of all, and there was Mia stuck on the top of the gate. Chitra, already over, was trying to help her down. As soon as she saw him, she ran for it, leaving Jack to assist his daughter over the gate.

He'd been unable to admonish her, so glad to find her unharmed.

He didn't believe that malarkey about a dare, but so what for now. Mia was back unharmed. He drove slowly home, so weary his body hardly seemed to belong to him. Only a short drive, thank heavens. He was blinking rapidly, what a long day...

He nodded off as he crossed the high street, waking in panic in the middle of Woodgrange Road. But the street was empty, nothing for him to hit, or to be hit by. Even so, he wasn't safe on the road. He pulled up once over the high street, and parked. It was only a few hundred yards to his front door. Do it on foot; driving he might nod off again, smash into something. And then have an assortment of problems.

He locked the van, taking twice as long as usual, and walked the rest of the way, the breeze slapping his face, keeping him awake for the few minutes it took.

Back home, he was disappointed to find Kim had left. He wondered where she'd gone, having quarrelled with her mother. Maybe she'd made it up, as daughters and mothers sometimes do.

Jack awoke at seven in the morning, on the sofa, fully dressed. Why not in bed, he couldn't recall, presumably where he'd dropped. He felt OK, a little stiff from the way he'd been lying, but three hours or so of sleep had refreshed him.

He'd get by.

Jack had a quick shower and put a plaster on the wound on the back of his hand. The last one he had; must get some more. He dressed in his work clothes. They could do with a wash. He should shower in them. For breakfast, he heated up the leavings of the Chinese takeaway. The remnants of his morning tea, from the teapot, he poured into his thermos with milk, made a cheese sandwich and was all set.

Mia was home, and he had work to do.

PART THREE:
DEATH AT THE CEMETERY

Chapter 28

Outside the cemetery, Jack took out his wheelbarrow from the van. He knew the rules, Mr Coe had made them plain enough yesterday. He couldn't park inside, so he needed to get everything out here or it would be a trek back for anything forgotten. It was bricklaying today. The footings should be firm, as he'd covered them with a plastic sheet from yesterday's rain. In the wheelbarrow, he put a bucket, a trowel, his long spirit level, a string line, line pins and a shovel. He thought for a few moments at what else he might need, and put in a club hammer and a bolster chisel as he'd likely need some half bricks.

He couldn't think of anything he'd missed, though there was bound to be something; there always was. So he locked up. Pushing the wheelbarrow through the open gate, he set off for his site in the cemetery. He'd phone Kim in a while, giving her time to get up as she would no longer be at work. A pity. He wanted to know where she'd gone last night. Sure, he'd been away for a couple of hours driving round looking for Mia, and maybe during that time Kim had contacted her mother. Patched things up.

Some quarrels are short lived.

Ruth Little, his client, was at the flower stall putting out plants on the trestle tables. She wore a floral housecoat, under it her thin legs were in tight jeans. Her face was gaunt, with make-up making her look almost ill. Her cheeks had been brought out in blusher, which didn't help, nor her very red lips. It was like stage make-up. He couldn't work out what she was trying to do, certainly not beautify herself. Though what did he know?

'Hello, Jack,' she said with a smile. Her teeth were fine, it was those red lips which took too much of his attention. Perhaps that was the point. 'How are you getting on up there?' she added.

'Quite well, Mrs Little.'

'Call me Ruth,' she said coyly. 'I'm not sure who Mrs Little is. I was Mrs Coe for 25 years, and then Ron died. And it didn't feel right staying Mrs Coe. But nor does Mrs Little. But I do run the Little Catering Company, so I have to own up to it sometimes. I'll respond to either if I have to. But I'd rather you just called me Ruth.'

'Ruth then,' he said with some difficulty. 'I laid the footings yesterday. That's the foundation for the brickwork. I hope to get the wall finished some time tomorrow. Then do the woodwork. Weather permitting of course.'

'I'll come up later when Nora gets here and have a look.' She shook her head. 'Kim does leave things untidy.'

'What is she like?' he said, knowing some of it and hoping to find out more.

Ruth threw up her hands. 'She had a quarrel with her mother. A big set to.' She sighed, then leaned in closer, almost whispering. 'It's difficult to work out whether Nora sacked her or Kim walked out. A lot of yelling and insults on both sides. Mothers and daughters, which one is worse?' She gave Jack a thin smile. 'Mind you, I always thought Kim a bit uppity for what she was. Did you know her husband was a gangster?'

'I did hear something about that,' he said carefully.

'In jail now, but that's another story.' She waved her hands. 'Scandal. Tabloid headlines. Money, women, drugs. He had his hands in everything and everyone. You know what I mean?' She smirked, adding, 'So Kim suited him. Good in bed, I expect. You know how it is. But that's not going to make a long term relationship. Is it?'

Jack didn't know what to say to this. Plainly Mrs Little didn't care much for Kim, and from what he knew of the meeting yesterday, that couldn't have improved things.

'She seemed nice to me,' he said.

Mrs Little patted him on the shoulder. 'All surface, Jack. All surface.' She waved a finger as a warning. 'She's a mean little madam. Nora took her back when her marriage collapsed, but it's all take and no give for Kim.'

'They could make up,' said Jack. 'Maybe they have already.'

'I'd be amazed if they do. You should hear Nora.' She held out an open hand. 'Do you want to place a bet on it? I'll take your cash any time.' She gave a shrill laugh, and settled back. 'I'm filling in for a day or two – but Nora will have to find someone soon as I've a big wedding coming up. I'm doing her a favour in the meantime. She's my sister-in-law and family should help family, but there are limits.'

Jack was thinking that Kim was family too, but kept it to himself. Family wars were best kept out of. Mrs Little was his employer and it was always advisable not to disagree. He knew when to shut up. At least when sober. Drunks lost the ability.

'I'd best get to work,' he said, looking up at the sky. 'Weather should be OK for the morning at least. So work while we can.' He found it hard to call her Ruth and so didn't. 'Bye for now.'

'Bye, Jack. I'll come up when I can.'

He lifted the wheelbarrow handles and pushed on, approaching the cars outside the crematorium, with floral tributes resting against the wall, but no people. Presumably inside, mourning another death. So much dying, it seemed. But then it was being here; this place collected them up, burnt them or buried them, attempting to do it in a neat and kindly manner. A send off with flowers and tears. Or a sigh of relief that the old bastard was underground, even if the tombstone said sadly missed.

The last lie.

His phone rang. Jack stopped with the wheelbarrow, just past the crematorium, and took out his phone. Alison. Would this be good or bad? He had brought Mia back, even if bearing some responsibility for her going off in the first place.

'Hello, Alison.'

'Good morning, Jack. Quite a night, wasn't it?'

'It certainly was. How's Mia?'

'Utterly knocked out. She's still in bed. I'm giving her the day off. But I've got to go to work. Milly next door is going to pop in from time to time. Can you come over?'

'I can come for my morning break, and for lunch. Do you still want me to do your ceiling?'

'Yes,' she said, 'but if you find a burglar, call the police.'

'Right,' he said, not wanting to open that argument. 'I'm at the cemetery now. I'll take a break about ten and come over.'

'You can make yourself a bacon sandwich. Mia'll probably still be in bed. Let her sleep.'

'Of course. Thanks for the sandwich offer. Best get to work.'

They ended the call. That was OK, he thought. Job still on and no reprimand. Daughter home and in bed, all going OK. He was still wide awake, but knew he'd suffer later. Let that happen when it did. And until then, work. Jack continued on his way. Conkers had come down again on the side road amid the curled brown leaves. He stopped, not being able to resist it, and picked up a conker, so bright and shiny, just out of its case. That glossy lustre as if freshly polished. It always went in a day, but for now, a good luck omen. He dropped it in the barrow and continued.

The cube of bricks was by the side of the road, along with the sacks of mortar. He threw one of the sacks in the wheelbarrow. He'd come back for bricks, he'd need water. There was a tap just ahead, just off the roadway, good.

Jack stamped his foot. Water reminded him; he'd left his thermos in the van again. Just too bad. He'd have to do without until he went over to Alison's for his tea break. He wasn't going to go all the way back to pick it up. Murphy's Law. Always something. Though why Murphy should get the blame...

He bumped up the path towards his site. From a distance he could see something wasn't right. The concrete was covered in the plastic sheet that he'd put over it yesterday to protect it from the downpour. But there was something on top. And the closer he came, dread thickened his throat, as it became clearer what that something was. A body, a woman's body.

Kim.

There was no doubt she was dead. The way her head was thrown back, mouth open, her arms splayed out, her skin white, with a bluish tinge. She was on her back, on the plastic sheet which had small puddles in its hollows. She was wearing the dress she'd been wearing last night, the denim jacket open, her chest covered in blood that had spilled on to the jacket and into the fabric of the dress. Her hair floated in a puddle behind her head like lank waterweed. The woolly hat he'd loaned her lay to one side.

Disbelief and fright disabled him. She had been with him last night, in his bed. She'd told him of her plans, made a will, they'd kissed, made love. His legs were weak and shaky. Tears welled.

Poor woman. How had this happened? She'd left him in the night, and ended up here. How did she get here? There was a snail on the side of her face; he removed it and threw it aside. He touched her cheek and forehead with his fingers.

No warmth, her face pallid, eyes wide open, reflecting the clouds. The universe had played a trick on him. He wasn't who he'd been two minutes earlier.

Jack knelt on the grass, a few feet from her. He took out his phone and dialled three numbers, waiting for a human voice.

Chapter 29

'What's the matter, Jack? You look like you've seen a ghost.'

Ruth had come out from behind the flower stall when she'd seen him approaching, somewhat wobbly. He could not reply, simply held out his phone to her. She took it and looked at the picture.

'That's Kim,' she exclaimed.

He took the camera, flicking through a few more pictures.

'I don't understand,' exclaimed Ruth in panic. 'What are you showing me?'

'She's dead,' he said, pointing back the way he'd come. 'There, at our site.'

Ruth screamed and ran across to the office. She went in and he watched through the long window as if at a silent movie. Ruth was all arms, waving this way and that, as she explained to Saul, both of them looking out at Jack who'd dropped onto a flower stall chair.

He was shivering, breathing rapidly. He knew it as shock, no less easier to deal with for recognising it. Kim was gone. A woman he was just beginning to know was dead. It had to be murder. He knew she hadn't been about to kill herself. She'd been making plans. She'd had so much to do today: find somewhere to live, start proceedings against Keith.

Keith. He'd said that he'd kill her. And Jack had given Kim that silly advice about writing a will. As if a bit of paper could protect her. He wiped his brow with the back of his hand, closed his eyes. He and she had walked arm in arm up his road, to and from Keith's, twice. First time, she'd been morose, when she'd found her brother-in-law in her house. But Kim had cheered up through the night. Written the will, gone back and dropped it off. They'd made love...

When he opened his eyes, Saul and Ruth were there. Saul in his earth brown suit and matching tie, frowning, with no choice but to speak to the builder.

'What's this about Kim?' he said.

'She's dead,' said Jack, handing him his phone.

Saul fiddled with the phone. 'I've lost it,' he said in annoyance.

Jack took the phone back and with Saul standing over his shoulder went through the four pictures he'd taken.

'She's lying at the site where I'm working,' he said as he flicked through. 'Cold as the morning dew.' Adding, as he came to the last picture, 'I've called the police.'

'That's not your prerogative,' declared Saul.

'She's dead,' he said.

'You just work here,' yelled Saul. 'I call the police!'

'Oh, you stupid man,' said Jack quietly. He didn't care, he might later, but couldn't imagine any later. 'She's dead. Murdered. I've called the police.'

Saul pointed to the cemetery gate. 'I want you out of here. You have no right speaking to me like that.'

He didn't move from the chair. 'The police will want to speak to me,' he said. 'They'll be here soon.'

Saul swivelled round to Ruth. 'You brought this buffoon here. Your insane memorial. And now see where we are.'

'I don't see what Ron's memorial has to do with Kim's death.' She was patting her eyes with a handkerchief. 'You were always against it. Jack's right. You are stupid.'

'I don't expect family support from you, Ruth.' He began to stride off. 'I'm going to check out this body.' He turned back for an instant and glared at Jack, as if he suspected Jack of making it up.

'Don't touch anything,' called Jack. 'It's a crime scene.'

He'd been told that over the phone. And all he could do was repeat it to Saul who was marching along, arms swinging, in the direction of the crematorium where mourners were exiting. Ruth was watching him too.

'He is a fool,' she said. 'Always making enemies, getting things out of proportion. I feel sorry for Sarah. She's got enough to deal with, without Saul adding to it.' She dabbed her eyes. 'Poor Kim. Whatever she's done, she doesn't deserve this. Poor you, finding her like that. I'm all aquiver. What a start to the day. I'll make us a cup of tea.'

There was a police siren from beyond the cemetery, some way off. It was real, now that he'd told people. Kim was dead. Everyone would see. She'd added to the busyness of the world. People were coming to deal with it. He would be peripheral with all the cops and police tape.

Chapter 30

Jack was seated on a bench, a little way up from the office and the flower stall. There was a cool breeze, fluttering the remaining leaves and bowing the top branches of the trees. He was shivery, somewhat outside himself, but recovering from the shock of his find, two hands round a mug of tea which retained a little warmth.

The bench was on a strip of close-cut lawn with an oval flower bed a little way up from him, containing a few languid roses. Beside him on the bench was Fayyad, his friend from the local police station, always smart in a suit and tie. His colleague DS Hayley Amis had borrowed a chair from the flower stall and was sitting facing them. She had a notebook and pen at the ready.

'That area up there is now a crime scene,' said Fayyad, indicating the direction of Jack's site. 'There's a constable on guard to keep people away, with chequered tape round to make it obvious. The crime scene investigators will be here shortly. You'll need to go to the station to give a full statement, Jack. But we'd like a preliminary chat to put us in the picture. That OK?'

'Fine.' He took a sip of tea. It was over-brewed and almost cold, but some comfort. His left knee was trembling; he had no control over it. It was less than half an hour ago that he'd found Kim and he was still coming to terms with the rearranged world.

'Tell us what you know about the victim,' said Fayyad.

'Apart from the fact that she's dead...' He put a hand up to acknowledge his attempt at humour was out of place. 'Sorry.

Her name is Kim. Kim Frank. That's her married name, but she's almost divorced. Her husband is Brad Frank.'

'The bank robber,' exclaimed Hayley.

'That's him,' said Jack.

'We know the Frank family,' said Fayyad. 'Too well.'

'She's been living with her mum, Nora Maxwell, for several months. Nora has the flower stall. Kim was working there, but she and her mother had a row yesterday, all to do with the board meeting.'

'What board?' asked Fayyad.

Jack realised Fayyad knew nothing. And hoped he could talk sense out of the jumble in his head, who she was, his relations with her, what he knew of her circumstances. Too much.

'The board of this place,' he said. 'The cemetery. They had a meeting in the office yesterday. You'll have to ask the others about the detail. All I know is Kim supported Saul Coe, the one her mother wasn't supporting. Don't ask me why Kim stood up for him. I can't stand the man. He's the self important gentleman in the brown suit in the office. They're all Kim's family. Saul is her uncle, David in the crematorium is another uncle. The lady over there at the flower stall, Ruth Little, is her aunt. They're all on the board of this place, and yesterday they had a blazing row.'

'How come you know all this, Jack?'

'Kim and I went out on a date last night. And she told me quite a bit. In fact, she couldn't stop talking about the awful meeting. I was thinking, this is going to be one lousy date. We were meant to be going out to dinner, but first we went to have a look at her house on Atherton Road. Turns out her brother in law, Keith Frank...'

'Oh, we know him too,' exclaimed Hayley.

'Well, he's squatting the place. And threatened to kill Kim if she tried to evict him.'

Fayyad and Hayley exchanged a look.

'We'll certainly follow that up, Jack.'

'Kim and I went to the Forest Gate police station straight after. So his threat's on record. That was about eight last night.'

'Good,' said Fayyad. 'That'll be at the station. Where did you go after that?'

'She wasn't in the mood for dinner out, so we went to my place on Earlham Grove. We ordered a takeaway from Moon House on Woodgrange Road. I ate most of it. Kim made a will giving everything to Battersea Dogs & Cats Home...'

'Why did she do that?'

'My dumb idea. I said it would say to Keith that if he killed her, the heir would still evict him. So murder would get him nowhere.'

'Makes sense,' said Fayyad. 'Not so dumb.'

'Feels dumb now.' He shrugged in a resigned way. 'Me and Kim took it round to the house late last night so he'd get it before he made any plans, dropped it through the letterbox. All signed, witnessed and dated. Then went back to my place. And to bed. At about twelve thirty, my ex wife phoned. My daughter, Mia, had gone missing...'

'Not the missing schoolgirl,' exclaimed Hayley, 'who went into the cemetery for a dare?'

'The very one,' said Jack.

'I heard it in the canteen this morning,' she said.

'You have been keeping us busy, Jack,' said Fayyad.

'It was never my plan,' he said. 'Where was I? The phone call from my ex. So, I left Kim in bed, went round to Alison's place, to find out about Mia going missing. And then I drove around Forest Gate for about an hour or more looking for her. Eventually finding her with a mate, Chitra, climbing over the cemetery gates to get out. Not that gate.' He flapped away the main gate they could see about thirty yards off. 'But the back gate.'

He was becoming aware of the complications. Finding the body, which made him a suspect. His daughter climbing out of the cemetery, his closeness to Kim last night, and the tangled tale of him leaving her and driving round Forest Gate.

'We'll need to have a chat with your daughter. Mia, is it?'

'Yeh. She's at home now. Day off school, because she's so whacked out. I'm off there when I've done with you, seeing I can't work here as my site is now a crime scene. Including my wheelbarrow and tools. Any chance I can get them back?'

'I'm afraid not.'

'I'd only just taken them up there.'

'The problem is that might be true or it might not be true.'

'I'm a suspect?'

Although he knew he was. How could he not be with all his involvement?

Fayyad shrugged. 'I'm afraid so, Jack. No one can be ruled out at this stage. But don't panic, we're not about to arrest you. So carry on with your story. You found your daughter, then what?'

'I took her home to her mum's. That's Alison Bell, she's a head teacher. There was a policeman there, so you can check on that. Then I went home to bed. And found that Kim had left.'

'What time did you get home?'

'About four in the morning. I collapsed and woke at seven on my sofa. Will that do you for starters?'

'For the time being. We'll need to do a lot of checking. But it's likely you were the last person to see Kim alive.'

'Apart from the murderer.'

'How long have you known her?'

'I first met her about nine o'clock yesterday morning. She gave me a cup of tea. And I last saw her twelve thirty this morning. That's...' He did a rapid calculation. 'Fifteen and a half hours. A brief affair.' His eyes welled, he dabbed them with the back of his hand.

Fayyad looked to Hayley who had stopped writing. Jack could guess what was in that look.

'Do I need a lawyer?'

'We're not charging you, Jack. I can't see any motive,' said Fayyad. 'But I'm just one cop. And pretty soon there's going to be a major incident team set up. You are the last known person to see the victim alive, and that puts you high on the suspect list. They'll go through your statement with a fine tooth comb. Check every bit of it that's checkable. But let's assume you're not the killer...' Hayley gave her colleague a warning look. 'Who do you think might've done it?'

Jack smiled ruefully. 'That's your job.'

'You can help out an old friend.' He grinned. 'I know you've a sharp eye.'

'Flattery, flattery... Let's have a think. There's Keith.'

'Definitely in the frame,' said Fayyad.

'And there's the whole family who own this cemetery between them. Saul, David, the two uncles. There's Nora, her mother, and Ruth, her aunt. That's a happy little crew. They had one hell of a row at their meeting yesterday and Kim was plumb in the middle of it. I'd have a chat with Maureen in the office, she was taking the minutes. She's the secretary or something like that. She'll put you in the picture.'

A sound of vehicles caused them to look to the gate. Two white vans were pulling in.

'Ah, the crime scene team,' exclaimed Fayyad. 'I'll take them up to the site.' He turned back to Jack. 'That'll do for now, mate. Give us Keith Frank's address. And then if you could go to Forest Gate Police Station this afternoon and make a full statement, I'd be grateful.'

Fayyad rose and set off to meet the vans, while Jack gave Hayley the address.

'Thanks, Jack,' she said, closing her notebook. She rose and went to join Fayyad who was talking to the driver of the first van.

'Just remembered something,' called Jack, snapping his fingers.

'What's that?' said Hayley, coming back to him.

'When I was driving round Forest Gate last night, looking for my daughter, I saw Saul Coe, the guy in the office there, must've been about three in the morning, he was driving down Hampton Road.'

'Could he have been coming from the cemetery?' She opened her notebook, made a jot and waited for his reply.

'He was only about quarter of a mile away. Why not?'

Chapter 31

Jack was by his van outside the cemetery, leaning on the engine. The scene of crime vans had gone in and disappeared from sight. Saul and Ruth were talking at the flower stall. From the gate, the cemetery appeared as normal. There was a funeral cortege at the crematorium, a leaf sweeper was sucking up fallen leaves. But then came a clue to something going on: a policeman in uniform was running up to the sweeper. He caught up with it and waved his arms wide. The machine stopped. It was like watching a silent movie. The leaf sweeper pulled to the side of the road and the driver got out.

There was to be no sweeping away of evidence.

Jack hardly knew what to do next, events had pummelled him. Today's work had been mapped out, until the discovery of the body. His site was now taken over by the police, he was a suspect and poor Kim was dead. He recalled, quite irrelevantly, she'd been going to the dentist today to have her teeth seen to. They'd be annoyed when she didn't show up. Would probably phone and write to her. Bill her perhaps.

There was the work at Alison's. The ceiling. Except nothing seemed important. Like a boxer floored after thirteen rounds, he didn't want to get up again and take more punishment.

Over at his site, beyond his view, busy people would be putting his tools into plastic bags, scouring the ground for anything dropped. Just as well they only had his bricklaying stuff. He didn't have much of that, but if such a job came up say tomorrow, he'd have to buy tools. Worry about that when he got the work, if he wasn't arrested for murder. His fingerprints would be all over the crime scene, but it couldn't be expected otherwise, he'd been working there yesterday. And who else would leave prints on his tools?

He was the last known person to see Kim alive. But he had no reason to kill her, they had to realise that. Unless he'd done a deal with the Battersea Dogs & Cats Home. And why would he be so stupid as to leave the body at his site? Which made him reflect why anybody would. Why there, of all places? She must have been killed sometime in the early hours. And surely at the site. The killer wouldn't drag a bleeding body around.

Pointless hanging round here, waiting for them to put the cuffs on him. He had to summon some energy, go to Alison's, see Mia, do the work on her ceiling. He had his hand on his door handle, but didn't move further for perhaps half a minute. He was turning the handle just as David was running through the wrought iron gates, his tie loose, collar button undone.

As he ran in, he shouted, 'Caught you, Jack.'

'How can I help?'

At his sloth speed, it was no effort for Jack to take his hand off the door handle and face the man.

David halted by him, catching his breath, 'What a to-do!' he exclaimed, hands on hips.

'Dreadful.'

'You found the body, I hear?'

'I did.'

'Any idea how she died?'

Was this simple curiosity, he wondered, before saying, 'There was a lot of blood. I didn't see any wounds. Stabbed, I should think. I've some horrible pictures if you'd like to see them.'

'Let's have a look,' said David.

Jack took out his phone and brought up the photos, then handed the phone to David who slowly went through the pictures. Ruth had almost jumped to the moon when he showed her the photos, but for David, they could have been holiday snaps.

'I agree on stabbing,' he said, handing Jack back the phone. 'I've seen a few.'

'You take it in your stride.'

David shrugged. 'I see corpses every day. It's sad to know Kim's dead, but a corpse is a corpse to me. I've seen bits of bodies that have been scraped off railway tracks, a man broken up and twisted by the blades of a dustcart, road accidents galore. Stab victims are, at least, in one piece. It's what happened before that's painful. The dying, not the corpse.'

'I've too much imagination,' said Jack. 'I see her alive at the flower stall.'

'Yes,' said David, wiping his brow with a tissue. 'Makes a difference when it's my niece. So young.' He sighed, still looking at a photo. 'I think my imagination is clicking in for once.' He handed back the phone. 'She was killed where you were working. Any idea why?'

'I've been wondering about that myself,' said Jack. 'And I can't make sense of it.' He threw up his hands. 'I mean, if you've stabbed someone in a graveyard, why not bury them?'

'Or cremate them,' said David.

'That'd be your thing. I couldn't work the machinery.'

Neither spoke for a short while, Jack niggling at the question of where the body had been found, his legs hollow, arms hardly belonging to him. The day was unreal. He was hardly in his body.

'I saw the cops talking to you,' said David. 'What did you say to them?'

'What I knew.'

He guessed this was why David had rushed over. He was fishing.

'What did that include?'

'About her family,' said Jack. 'You lot. I told them who was who. As much as I knew anyway. I told them about the row you had at your meeting yesterday...'

'You told them about that?'

'Kim told me about it,' he said. 'The big family blow up.'

'I'd rather hoped that wouldn't get out,' said David. 'Bound to, I suppose. Now they'll be all over us. You weren't to know. I'd better have a word with the others.' He scratched his thinning hair. 'This is an awful mess.'

'I liked her,' said Jack. 'She was a nice woman.'

'Not always so nice,' said David. He bit his lower lip, looking through the gates into the graveyard. 'I wonder what the cops are finding up there.' He turned back. 'What you going to be doing today? They've taken over your site.'

'I've some work up the road. Nothing much. But I hardly feel like working anyway. I will though, take it slow. It keeps me sane when crazy things happen. I don't know when I'll get back here. They've got some of my tools. Anyone would think she was hit with a shovel.'

Chapter 32

Jack arrived at Alison's. He'd missed the school run and so was able to park outside her house. One blessing, if it was worth counting. Just eight hours ago, he'd been telling Kim how he'd like to learn more about architecture. They'd been within a snap of making love when Alison phoned. If Alison hadn't, maybe Kim wouldn't have left.

Why had she?

He had the key from yesterday and opened Alison's front door. There were no sounds of life in the passage, unlike yesterday. Mia must still be in bed. He'd best check on her. He went upstairs and quietly looked into her room. It was tidy, Alison insisted she kept it in a reasonable state. A poster of the moons of Jupiter was on the wall, along with one from a Harry Potter movie. Mia was a bundle of bed-clothing, utterly covered up. To reassure himself, he checked she was in there. Yes, in her pyjamas, in foetal position, fast asleep.

He left her and went downstairs. If he started working, he'd wake her. Better she slept. He'd make himself a sand-wich and a cup of tea. No rush. Get his gear in the house ready for work. Phone Alison, tell her he was here. Do that first.

He rang her.

'Hello, Jack.'

'I'm at your place,' he said.

'How's Mia?'

'Fast asleep. I can't work at the cemetery today, they've found a body.'

'That shouldn't be difficult, in a cemetery.'

'Someone was murdered there,' he said. 'So it's a crime scene. Killed last night. The cops want to interview Mia as she was there.'

'What a palaver, last night! Do you believe that tale about a dare?'

'I saw her climbing out, so she was certainly there,' he said. 'What she was actually doing, I'll ask her when she wakes up. The cops think she might have seen something.'

'You'll be with her at the interview?'

'I will. I don't suppose she'll have much to tell them. I'll take her to the cop shop this afternoon. This morning, I'm going to take your ceiling down.'

'Cover everything, please.'

'Don't worry. I have done this before.'

'Famous last words. Must go, I've a parent waiting. Might see you later.'

And she closed the call. Jack sighed with relief. That was done. He'd told her that he had to go to the police station, but not that he knew the victim. Or was a suspect. It was always best with Alison to tell her as little as necessary. The problem was judging exactly what that was.

He'd have a bite to eat. Take it at a snail's pace. No rush with just this work to do.

Jack put the kettle on and took some bacon slices out of the fridge, and threw them in a frying pan. As they fried, he got bread and a plate out on the table. Alison always had seedy, wholemeal bread. He found it a bit of a crunch, but it was all there was. Healthy stuff.

He flipped the bacon on to the plate with a spatula. And stopped, a rise of vomit in his throat. The colour of the bacon reminded him of Kim, the blood on her chest, the pinkish brown. He took a drink of water, washed out his mouth. He stood shivering, glanced at the bacon on the plate, thought for an instant of saving it for Mia, but the sight of it caused his stomach to heave. He threw it quickly in the bin.

The very smell was revolting. He opened the kitchen window and washed out the pan, but the smell stuck around, fried flesh, pinkish, greasy brown. He made tea, just a teabag in a cup with milk. And considered whether he should work at all today, he was so shaky. But then what else would he do? Sit around watching daytime TV, with too much time to think about the body at the site. He'd hardly known her. And yet knew her well. Kim had a beautiful laugh, her hand would go to her face to hide the gap in her teeth. She could get very angry, then switch in a moment. The things she'd told him, her plans for a coffee shop, about her family and her husband. He'd persuaded her to make that dumb will.

All gone.

He'd learnt a lot about her in just a few hours. Would there have been any future for them as a couple? Who can ever say? The time they had, they got on well. Could talk, hadn't had a row, though hardly had the time for one. She listened, she didn't criticise.

She was dead.

Jack looked up at the ceiling. The centre patch around the light was stained and sagging. The water damage probably crossed two plasterboards, but could be patched in half of one. With luck, he could cut out the damaged section with not too much mess. That would keep Alison happy. Then leave the joists to dry out for a couple of weeks before putting new board in, plastering over and painting the ceiling. A simple job, to be done in stages.

He went out to his van, and took out a couple of decorating sheets, a hammer, bucket, cold chisel, and plaster saw. He searched for his long spirit level, remembering, after a futile hunt, that the cops had it. He'd have to get by with the short one.

Jack brought everything into the house, leaving them in the hall outside the kitchen. He'd decided to use Alison's ladder, rather than his own. He went upstairs to get it, as Mia was coming out of the bathroom.

'What you doing here, Dad?' she said rubbing her eyes.

She was in her pyjamas, a pattern of flying kites. Her hair was tousled, thick and curly, face bleary.

'Fixing your ceiling,' he said. 'Do you want breakfast before I get started?'

'OK. Let me get my dressing gown.'

She went into her bedroom. Jack took the ladder downstairs, and left it in the hallway with his gear. In the kitchen, he could still smell the salty, acrid smell of fried bacon, the colour coming back to him. Would he ever be able to eat it again?

Mia joined him in a few minutes. She sat at the table, quite washed out, in her dressing gown with the soaring seagulls, and bare feet. Her mother would have insisted on her brushing her hair at least, but he figured it didn't matter at all. He was glad of the company.

'What would you like to eat?' he said, hoping she'd say anything except bacon.

She considered for a few moments, so vulnerable in her dressing gown and bare feet. He thought of her in the graveyard, with a murderer prowling around. He shuddered. An awful image.

'Boiled egg,' she said.

Jack, grateful for her choice, set to making toast and three boiled eggs. He figured he could manage one himself. Mia made the coffee. Alison had a coffee grinder and cafetiere, which Mia was more in tune with than Jack who had instant at home, but could tell the difference.

He was impatient to question her about last night, but best get her comfortable. Have breakfast together, chat as if all were normal. So they talked about school. There was a trip to France in spring that Mia wanted to go on. That was fine by him, certainly would be no problem with Alison. Though he'd need to fork out half the cash. Maybe he'd suggest that Alison paid for it, in exchange for the ceiling work. Except he could do with the money now, not knowing when the cemetery job would get going again.

His egg was runny, he could stomach it if he ate slowly. The toast was fine. Mia ate like an innocent, which her father didn't believe one bit. We all have our sins.

'About last night,' he said.

'I wondered when we were going to come to that.'

She'd cut her toast into soldiers and was dipping one in the egg.

'Was it really a dare?'

'Yes,' she said, very intent on eating.

'Strange dare.'

She looked up at him. 'If it wasn't strange, it would hardly be worth doing.'

'But you hadn't seen Chitra in ages,' he said.

'I contacted her through friends,' she said. 'And we talked about this and that. People we knew. And she made this dare. I had to sit on a gravestone for an hour at midnight.'

He still didn't believe her, but said, 'Was there a prize?'

'Yes,' she said. 'I bet my teddy bear bracelet.'

'What did she bet?'

She thought for a second, then said, 'Ten pounds.'

He was impressed. A clever lie, as he'd given Chitra a tenner. Though should he be impressed?

'Who won?'

'I did.'

This was fruitless. He wasn't going to get any further without beating it out of her, and he certainly wouldn't do that. To what end? But the two girls had been in the cemetery. That was not deniable as he'd caught them climbing out.

'There was a murder in the cemetery last night,' he said.

'You're joking!' she said, aghast.

'A woman was killed. Probably stabbed. That's why I'm here. Where I was working is a crime scene.'

'Like on TV,' she said, excited by the idea of murder and the police. 'They gather up whatever they find and put it in plastic bags.'

'They do,' he said, wondering how much detail he should give her. Some was necessary. 'I found the body when I went to work. A woman's,' he went on. 'So I phoned the police.'

'You found the body!' Thoroughly awake now. 'What was it like?'

'Covered in blood. Horrible.' He wouldn't show her the photos.

'I bet it was.'

'I was questioned by the police.' He wasn't going to tell her he knew the victim. Too complicated. 'They want to talk to you.'

'What about?'

'You were there,' he said, 'with Chitra. Your dare. Did you see anyone?'

She'd stopped eating, half her toast soldiers on the plate, one egg shell empty, the other in the Humpty Dumpty cup, cracked at the top. She'd hesitated too long.

'You did,' he said. 'Who?'

'A man and a woman,' she said cautiously. 'They went into the office. I didn't know who they were. But Chitra recognised them.'

He was alerted.

'That could be vital,' he said.

Chapter 33

It was cramped in the flower stall hut with the three chairs and occupants in amongst pots and sacks of compost. Hayley and Fayyad were interviewing Nora. She wore a bright, crimson dress, revealing ample cleavage, hardly flattering with her weeping and sniffing.

'You were angry with your daughter after the meeting,' said Fayyad.

'So angry I could have knocked her head off…' A hand flew to her puffed face. 'Sorry, sorry, what am I saying!' She sniffed and dabbed her eyes with a handkerchief. 'I can't believe she's dead. My Kim. I kicked her out, you know. Temper, I have a terrible temper. It put paid to my marriage. Not that it was worth salvaging.'

'Why did you need to win the vote at the meeting?'

She took a deep breath. 'I shouldn't be saying this, but I suppose I have to.' She wiped her eyes again. 'My make-up must be an awful mess. Who cares! What was I saying? The meeting, the vote. Some of us, that's me, David and Ruth, had worked out a plan to sell off about an acre of the cemetery for new-build housing. But Saul wouldn't have it. He doesn't need money, Sarah had her mammoth pay off for her accident… But we do. And it's unfair of him to have so much say. He wants to wait a few years, take advantage of the rising market. But who says it will keep rising? And we need the cash now.' She stopped her roll. 'I can show you the draft plan. You'll see the sense of it. It wouldn't make the cemetery that much smaller.'

'What do you need the money for, Nora?'

'I want a shop. A sizeable shop. Not some silly thing that'll go bust in three months, but in an affluent area, selling to the well off. At the lower end shops can't compete with the internet or the chains. But the high end customers are not concerned with price; they want the brands, the quality. I can't go running round to car boot sales much longer, selling off my market stalls. I'm getting too old for that. But to do what I want to do needs money. A lot of money. And Kim sided with Saul and his cronies. He must have bought her vote, I tell you. I can't think of any other reason. I was so angry with her. I kicked her out. I thought, if she's going to come back home, the very least she can do is support me.'

Her eyes filled with tears. She covered her face in her hands.

'I didn't know this was going to happen. Had no idea. Excuse me, excuse me.' She was wiping her eyes, her make-up smeared. 'She's very difficult, I'm very difficult. I can be a bully, I know it, I've been told. I should go in for temper management...'

She continued wiping her eyes, her body heaving.

'We could do this another time,' said Fayyad. Hayley nodded.

'No, no,' exclaimed Nora. 'I want you to catch whoever did it. And it wasn't me. I would never do a thing like that. I am all noise. I was sorry I'd had a go at her two hours later. That's me all over.'

'You said why you needed the money, but what about David and Ruth? What do they need it for?'

'You'll have to ask David about his gambling. He's a fool. And he's got some woman on the go. Always has someone. He tries to live the high life. Talk to him about where the money comes from.'

'And Ruth?'

'She made some poor investments. She's all right, I think. You can never be sure with Ruth. Paying that builder to do her memorial for her husband; she must have some spare cash. Though maybe that job's just to annoy Saul. And could be done with borrowed money. You'll have to ask her.'

'We will,' said Fayyad. 'Can you tell us about last night? What you did?'

'After the meeting, Ruth and David came to my place. We talked about what to do. How to handle Kim.' She looked about her, as if someone might hear. 'David suggested we pay her more than Saul was coughing up.'

'What did you think of that?'

'I didn't like it. Money for nothing. She's always had money for nothing, including that house she's just got.' She leaned in. 'Do you know what's happening to it?'

'You'll have to wait for the will, Nora.'

'So there is a will. Any idea what it says?'

'You don't know?'

'I don't.' She threw her hands up. 'See what I'm like? She's just died. My only daughter. Murdered. And I'm already thinking of her will, and whether I'll get anything. Do you know what it says?'

'I've not seen the will,' said Fayyad. 'Simply heard there is one. And I can't say any more on that. You were telling us about the meeting at your place. How long did it go on for?'

'Ruth and David left about nine thirty. Then I did some accounts for about an hour. After that, I sorted out vintage clothing for the next day on my Hackney stall. I've had to cancel that. How could I not?' She wiped her eyes and sniffed several times. 'Sorry... I went to bed about twelve thirty. But I was woken up, just after one o'clock. It was Kim. I was amazed. One o'clock in the morning! What a time to phone. She said we didn't have to be enemies. She was going to rent a flat in Stratford. She wanted to set up a business, a coffee shop. That was the first she'd told me of it.'

Nora broke off in tears, body shaking. Fayyad looked to Hayley, who signalled to leave her.

'She told me her plans,' she said at last. 'She said we don't have to be enemies...' She wiped her eyes. 'Sorry, sorry. But as usual, it finished in a quarrel. I said some things, she said some things. I called her a gangster's tart.' She looked to Fayyad and Hayley in distress. 'Imagine, the last thing I said to my only daughter. You're a gangster's tart.' Her body heaved and shook, her face bruised and red. 'I should be hanged, drawn and quartered.'

Fayyad glanced at Hayley and pointed at his watch. Hayley nodded. Nora was wiping her face with a wet handkerchief, gasping.

'Thank you, Nora, for what you've told us,' said Fayyad. 'You'll need to give a full statement at Forest Gate Police Station as soon as possible. I'll get someone to drive you there.' He leaned forward, gently patting her hand. 'We appreciate the information you've given us. We know this is distressing, but, believe me, we are doing all we can to catch the killer. Have you any thoughts who it might be? Someone in the family perhaps?'

'No! None of us would do anything like that. David or Saul or Ruth might shout, rant and rage. But murder? It's not in our nature. We're business people. You look to her husband, Brad. His brother, Keith. Scum of the earth. That would be my first port of call. Take a shotgun.'

Chapter 34

Jack moved the tables and chairs from the kitchen into the sitting room. China and cutlery he put away in cupboards and drawers. The oven and fridge he covered with a sheet along with the working surfaces, the floor too, grateful that Alison couldn't see the state of the sheets. They'd be back in the van by the time she got back. He must wash them. It was never a priority.

Putting up the stepladder, he climbed to the ceiling and examined the bulging plasterboard. He felt it with his fingers; it was soggy in the centre. All the wet stuff would have to be cut out. He needed the spirit level to test where the plasterboard was flat again and hadn't been water damaged. His long spirit level had been picked up on the crime scene; he'd have to work with the smaller one.

Over the next half hour, working with the spirit level, Jack pencilled out a large square on the ceiling, the area that had to be cut out and replaced. About 1.2 metres square. Convenient; it meant he wouldn't be working with a full board when it came to replacement. Always tricky to handle on his own, though he'd developed a way of working using props.

As he cut out the water damaged board with his thin plaster-saw, he returned, like an itching pimple, to the fact that was irritating him. Why was Kim's body on his site? It couldn't just be coincidence. It made him a suspect. Maybe someone was trying to frame him. If so, it had to be one of the family. Certainly he got on badly with Saul Coe, but didn't everyone? Saul didn't want him doing the job at all. But a murder was a drastic way of stopping it.

Then there was David. Seemed a decent guy; he'd treated Jack's wound, shown him round the crematorium, given him a cup of tea. He couldn't see any motive there, but might be missing something. There was Kim's mother. She was in constant warfare with her daughter. But murder? And why draw him into it? As for Ruth Little, now working at the flower stall, she was his customer, had paid him half the money. She was a bit flirty, but so what?

It had to be one of the family.

Could his relationship with Kim have anything to do with it? Saul would have seen them chatting at the flower stall. Would her mother have seen them? He couldn't recall; he hadn't been looking. And why should it bother anyone? Only a first date, it could fizzle out in a week.

Jack recalled Kim saying Saul had tried it on with her once. Men hate being rejected. He knew that from his own experience. Could that be the key?

He was going round in circles. But the body, where it was found, had to be a factor.

The water damaged board, he was able to remove in a few large pieces, which was all to the good, as being damp it held together with little dust. Once the cutting was done, the square in the ceiling was tidy, the joists showing and the wooden crosspieces on which the plasterboard had been screwed. Above the joists were the bathroom floorboards. He'd had to take care with the wiring and light fitting, but all in all, a good job. Neat and square, making it easy to put in the replacement in a couple of weeks.

From the top of the ladder, with a sponge and paper kitchen towels, Jack wiped off as much moisture as he could from the joists and bathroom floorboards. Finishing that, he came down the ladder. The job was done for the time being, apart from the clearing up. He'd give it two weeks to dry out thoroughly, then come back, put new board in, plaster it to match the rest of the ceiling. And then a coat or two of paint over the whole ceiling.

He deserved a cup of tea. Take one up to Mia who was in her bedroom reading. Then clear up the debris. Get the tools and sheets back in the van. And maybe a walk in West Ham Park before going to the police station.

Chapter 35

Hayley and Fayyad were parked outside Keith's place. He was thankful Hayley was with him. They were a good team; she was sharp, but just as important, she had a black belt in judo. A great comfort when interviewing suspects like Keith, who could blow up in an instant.

'What did you think of Nora?' he said.

'She's very distressed,' said Hayley. 'I didn't think she was putting it on, but you never can tell.'

'I did wonder,' said Fayyad. 'Was she suffering for Kim, or for herself?'

'Would she really murder her daughter?'

'Rule nothing out at this stage, as the boss says,' he said with a shrug, referring to Detective Superintendent Nikki Martin who was in charge of the investigation.

'She's texted us,' said Hayley. 'We have our first incident meeting at three.'

'See if we can get it solved by then,' he said with a grin. 'Big boy here might have some answers. Let's go.'

They locked the car, and went to the front door. Fayyad rang the bell. While they waited for the response, he straightened his tie and jacket.

'Stay polite,' he said. 'Keith Frank can be touchy. I've interviewed him before. He took a swing at a constable. I can't even remember what for. Something he just didn't like.'

'Let him try,' said Hayley. 'I'm ready.'

Keith came to the door, his broad body taking up much of the frame. He was in a half sleeved white polo top, biceps bulging, his beige chinos had a keen crease. Fayyad found it difficult not to stare at his bald head.

'Detective Sergeant...' Keith flicked his fingers. 'Don't tell me.' He snapped his fingers again then shook his head. 'I'm no good with foreign names.'

'Kamani,' said Fayyad, thinking it unimportant to inform Keith he was born in Newham General Hospital.

'Detective Constable Amis,' added Hayley, watching Keith closely.

'And what do I owe the pleasure of this visit?'

'I'm sorry to have to inform you that your sister in law has been murdered, Mr Frank.'

'Which one?' He was suddenly alert.

Fayyad wondered how many sisters in law he had. How many might be threatened with murder.

'Kim,' he said.

'Kim? You've got to be joking.'

'I'm afraid not. May we come in, we've some questions for you.'

Keith pushed out his arms to both doorjambs, daring them to push past. 'I'm rather busy at the moment.'

'This won't take long, Mr Frank. The alternative is a visit to the police station.'

Keith hissed, and didn't reply for a few seconds.

'Come in,' he said huffily.

He led them along the hallway and into a sitting room where there was a young woman with a toddler.

'Police,' he said to her. 'Nothing serious, but if you could make us a cuppa...'

'Not for me,' said Fayyad. 'Thank you.'

'Nor me,' said Hayley.

The woman hurried out with the child. The room had new furniture: a light brown leather sofa with two matching armchairs, a large flat screen TV and music centre. There were photos on the mantelpiece that Fayyad would have liked to have a closer look at. On the carpet were children's toys.

Keith offered Hayley and Fayyad the sofa while he took an armchair.

'So Kim's been topped,' he said.

'I'm afraid so,' said Fayyad. 'And you had some sharp words with her yesterday.'

'That bloke she was with, he been telling you?'

'You threatened to kill her if she made any attempt to evict you.'

Keith smiled broadly. 'Total bluster. You know how it is.' He play acted a jocular threat, 'Do whatever and I'll knock your block off.' And laughed. 'Pure banter. Nothing mean in it.'

'She owned this property,' said Fayyad. 'And she didn't want you here.'

'You've got that wrong,' said Keith. 'My brother owns it.'

'It's in her name.'

Keith shrugged. 'Tax purposes. You know how it works.'

Fayyad didn't. He'd leave that to the experts.

'She was in the process of divorcing your brother,' he said. 'And if a property is in her name, then it's hers.'

Keith didn't reply. Fayyad could see by his gritted teeth that he'd angered him. He was glad Keith was sitting down. He'd have to rise for a blow, making it easier to evade or for Hayley to move in quickly. Having seen her in action, he almost hoped Keith would try something.

'OK. I said some words to her,' admitted Keith, 'which I now regret. I've lived here with my family for nearly two years. And she comes to the door and says she wants me out. Who wouldn't lose their temper?'

'Temper is understandable,' said Fayyad. 'But you threatened to kill her if she took any action.'

Keith threw up his hands. 'A waste of time.' He rose and went to the mantelpiece. 'Look what she gave me.' He handed over a folded piece of paper.

Fayyad and Hayley rapidly read it. A will.

'This house now belongs to the Battersea Dogs & Cats Home,' said Keith. 'It wouldn't do me any good killing her.'

'They'll evict you, once they know you are here,' said Fayyad. 'Give you notice. Do it by the law, but they'll evict you.'

Keith sighed and gestured around the room. 'Nice house. I like it here. Gym just up the road. Good for shopping for the missus, with Stratford ten minutes away. I hope they're slow about it. Committees and all that. But anyway, you haven't come to help me with my housing. It's just with that will, and me knowing what was in it – what would be the point of me bumping her off?'

'When did you get this?'

'It came through the letterbox about eleven last night.'

'I'll keep it as evidence,' said Fayyad. He'd noted the witness signature, Jack Bell, fitting with what Jack had told him.

'Keep it,' shrugged Keith. 'I don't need it here to remind me. Have this as well.'

He handed over a brief letter, saying a copy had been lodged with her solicitor. It was signed by Kim. He passed them to Hayley.

'Thank you for the papers,' said Fayyad. 'And for the record, Mr Frank, where were you last night after eleven o'clock?'

'Here, officer. Never left the house. You can ask the missus. I'll call her for you.'

Fayyad and Hayley left a few minutes later. His wife confirmed Keith had been in the rest of the night. For what that was worth.

Chapter 36

'You OK now?' asked Jack.

'Yeh, I think so. The lie-in did me good,' said Mia.

'Then maybe you should go to school this afternoon,' he half teased.

'I mean, I'm OK in the fresh air,' she said. 'I could easily fall asleep in class.'

They were in West Ham Park. Wet leaves lay on the tree-lined path they were walking down. Approaching them, a noisy machine, containing a man in overalls, was sucking them up. They stepped aside to let it go past. The man lifted a hand to acknowledge them. Jack gave him a nod, remembering him from past visits.

They turned at the sound of a whistle, to see a teacher yelling and boys in shorts on a field forming a ragged line.

'What school's that?' he said.

'Don't know,' said Mia. 'There's a lot round here. St Angela's, St Bon's, Stratford school – and that's just the secondaries. Our school comes here sometimes, but up the other end of the park.'

A jet plane was low in the sky, heading for London City Airport in the south of the borough. The sky was lively with birds, white clouds scurrying across the blue. It might just clear, and if so a night out with the telescope was due.

Jack considered pressing Mia about the dare story, but thought better of it. They were off to Forest Gate police station after the walk, and the police would ask her anyway. He had his own statement to give. This time, he must add that Kim had told him that she'd had trouble with Saul trying it on. So much to remember, easy to forget something. He wondered how much of a suspect he was when it came down to it. No money to be gained, no sexual jealousy, he'd hardly known her, whereas her family had motives by the bucketful. He smiled to himself; the family had yet to learn about the will and the beneficiary, Battersea Dogs & Cats Home.

'What you smiling at, Dad?'

'It's a nice day for a stroll,' he said. 'Birds singing. There's a squirrel watching us. Just there. I've fixed your ceiling for the time being. I'm having a pleasant walk with my daughter. What's not to smile at?'

'They're going to question me,' she said. 'You found a body.'

How could he block it out so easily? But he had. Sunshine, squirrels, birds, fluffy clouds. And yes, he found a body. Kim's. Someone had murdered her. He had liked her, slept with her. Had little sleep, was that sufficient excuse?

Mia was in blue jeans and a red sweater on which Mary Poppins floated down with her umbrella. Over it she wore an unzipped jacket. Jack was in overalls and a light jacket, work clothes as he hadn't been home. The cops would have to take him as he was.

'Just tell the truth,' he said. 'You've nothing to hide. Have you?'

'Nothing,' she said.

She picked up a conker and threw it at the squirrel. And, of course, missed.

'Who was the woman who got killed?' she said.

'She worked on the flower stall at the cemetery.'

'Did you know her?'

She threw another conker, while he considered whether to lie or not.

'I did.'

She turned to him. 'Did you go out with her?'

'What's this, a police grilling?'

'That was a simple question,' she said, sounding just like her mother.

'I did,' he said. 'Once.' True as far as it went.

She threw another conker at the squirrel which was now in the fork of a tree.

'Did you like her?'

'I did. And please don't ask me any more questions. I'm upset she was murdered.'

'Sorry, Dad.'

'I took her out last night,' he said, 'for the first and last time. And I liked her.'

'Someone killed her after she left you.'

'Change the subject.'

They were silent. That was bruising. Though what did he have to feel guilty about? He was single, Kim had been, more or less. But if he hadn't left her in the early hours, for which his daughter was responsible, who knows? Then again, if he'd called the police on Chitra for burglary, then she'd have been taken into some sort of care, his daughter wouldn't have crept out, and Jack would have stayed at home cuddling up with Kim. Alternative universes, different paths taken.

'You were in love with Mum once,' said Mia.

'I was,' he admitted.

'So where did that go?'

She was circling the tree, watching the squirrel, a conker at the ready.

'Your mum is ambitious,' he said. 'I think she regretted marrying a builder.'

Mia turned on him. 'You kept getting drunk, you mean,' she exclaimed. 'You were awful.'

'I was,' he said. 'I'm sorry for the trouble I caused.'

He sat on a bench; Mia had been old enough to remember his drunken days. Apologise, said his group, Alcohol Halt, for the trouble you've caused. He had been awful, he was sure, though being drunk couldn't recall much of it.

Mia was rounding the tree slowly. He wished she'd stop tormenting the squirrel.

'You nearly set the house on fire,' she said, turning on him. 'With a candle by your bed.'

'I don't remember.'

'That's because you were drunk.'

He struck back at her. 'I don't believe you went on a dare last night.'

She turned, a hateful stare.

'You don't have to. It's the police that count. Not you.'

Chapter 37

Saul was seated behind the dark brown desk in his office, almost a perfect match for his customary suit and tanned face. Fayyad and Hayley were in chairs in front. Maureen had offered tea; they'd declined. There was a lot to do today. The first 24 hours in an investigation were the most important, before memories got vague and evidence was disposed of.

'How did you get on with your niece?' asked Fayyad.

'Pretty well,' said Saul, scratching his thinning hair. 'She supported me at the board meeting, you know.'

'I do,' said Fayyad. 'Did you pay her for that?'

'Of course not.'

'It has been suggested that you did.'

Saul waved a finger of accusation. 'Who by? Not that brother of mine, he'd say anything to put me down.' He stopped, he sighed. 'I discussed the matter with Kim. She saw it was not the time to sell off any of the cemetery or change the board structure.' He squeezed his nose. 'She was a very reasonable young lady. You cannot believe how hurt I am by her death.'

Fayyad had noted Saul's agitation. Police interviews sometimes had that effect, often indistinguishable from guilt. Though grief couldn't be ruled out. Keep an open mind, as the boss said too often.

'You were out late last night, Mr Coe,' said Fayyad. 'Why?'

'I don't sleep well,' he said. 'Sarah has bad dreams; they're hard to take. She has 24 hour care. I go for a drive sometimes to calm myself down. And yesterday, on top of everything, was the meeting. I'm sure you've heard about it.'

'We have,' said Fayyad, taking care not to lose his train of thought. 'In the early hours, you were seen driving, near the cemetery.'

'Who told you that? That builder? He was out last night himself. Ask him what he was doing.'

'We have done, Mr Coe. But please answer my question. Did you go to the cemetery late last night?'

Saul brushed back his hair. 'No. Is that good enough for you? I was out driving to calm myself down. That's not illegal, is it?'

'Not at all, Mr Coe. Though when you were seen, you were driving fast. Why was that? One doesn't do that to calm down.'

Saul was rapping his fingers on the desk, a tidy top, empty of everything but a calendar.

'I received a phone call while I was out,' he said. 'Sarah was having a fit. You can check that with Badrah, the carer on duty. As it happened, it wasn't serious. But how was I to know? An ambulance was called, you can check that too. But it wasn't needed.'

'So you didn't go to the cemetery?'

'No. How many times do I need to tell you?'

'Where did you go?'

'I was out for about an hour.' He sighed heavily, emphasising his annoyance at the questioning. 'I drove up the Woodford New Road. As far as Epping. Then turned back.'

Fayyad considered this. A drive out, late at night, no witnesses. They might check CCTV footage if necessary, to see if his car was where he said it was. There was nothing to be gained by further questions on this topic. Not at the moment.

'Do you recognise this?' Fayyad placed a dark red pen in a plastic bag on the desk. 'It has your name engraved on it.'

'It's my pen,' said Saul. 'A Schaeffer.'

'It was found under the body. Do you have an explanation for that?'

Saul hesitated, began to say something then stopped himself.

'I want to see a solicitor,' he said. 'I'm not saying any more without a solicitor present.'

'That's your right,' said Fayyad. 'We'll continue this interview at Forest Gate Police Station. It will be recorded. For your protection. To save time, I suggest you phone your solicitor now.'

Chapter 38

Jack and Mia were in a small interview room. Across the table from them were a middle aged woman, obviously the senior, and a slim man in his twenties. She wore a navy dress suit, smart, he less so, in a grey suit with trousers that could do with ironing.

The woman said, 'Hello, Mia.' She had short fair hair and wore no make-up.

'Good afternoon, madam,' said Mia, avoiding the police officer's eye. She went to a girls' school where the women teachers were addressed as madam.

'I am Detective Superintendent Nikki Martin. Do you know what a detective superintendent is, Mia?'

'It's a high up policeman...' she said, then quickly retracted, 'I mean police officer.'

'Well done, Mia.' She smiled. 'A lot of my officers don't see the distinction. I can tell you're a bright girl. This is my colleague, Detective Constable John Wharton.'

'Hello, Mia.' He gave her a friendly smile.

'Hello, sir.'

'We're not here to arrest you or anything like that, Mia,' said DS Martin. 'We just want information.'

'I understand, madam.'

'We are recording this interview. That's so it's on record. It also means I must treat you reasonably or I'm in trouble. Do you understand?'

'Yes, madam.'

'Good. You've got your father with you, and that's fine. We're not here to bully you or press you into saying something you don't want to say.' Mia nodded. DS Martin continued. 'So let's begin. You were in the cemetery last night, Mia. Can you tell me why?'

Mia took a deep breath. Jack was watching her closely. Plainly Mia was intimidated by the people and the place. He hoped she could handle it.

'It was a dare,' she said, taking a glance at Jack. 'A stupid dare. I had to sit on a grave for an hour.'

'And who gave you the dare, Mia?'

'Chitra. Chitra Bhatti. She used to go to my school, Sarah Bonnell. She was with me.'

And helped you set up the story, thought Jack.

'I'm with you so far, Mia,' said DS Martin. 'You and Chitra were in the cemetery. What sort of time was this?'

'We went in about quarter past eleven,' said Mia.

Jack would have liked to have intervened. He'd found her around 3 am. Almost four hours later!

'What time did you find her, Mr Bell?'

'A little before three,' said Jack.

'Four hours in the graveyard, Mia. Why so long for a one hour dare?'

Jack was pleased she'd picked up on this.

'Oh, we messed around a lot before the dare, telling ghost stories and the like. We had some picnic stuff.'

'Odd place for a picnic.'

'That's why we did it.'

Jack was surprised at her boldness. Clearly she'd accepted that she wasn't in trouble. And DS Martin was working at being unthreatening.

'Did you see anyone while you were in the cemetery?'

'Yes,' she said carefully. 'A man and a woman. We hid behind the flower hut, and saw them go into the office.'

'What time was this?'

'I can't be sure. I didn't have a watch. I left my phone at home.'

'Give me an estimate.'

'Somewhere around two o'clock. Maybe two thirty. About twenty minutes before Dad came...'

'And what time was that, Mr Bell? Be as exact as you can.'

'Ten to three.'

'Thank you.' She turned to Mia. 'What can you tell us about this man and woman, Mia?'

'The man wore a short coat,' she said. 'He was quite old, about as old as you are. The woman was younger and wore a woolly hat.'

'Had you seen them before, Mia?'

'No.'

'I've some photos here. I'd like you to look at them.'

From a folder she took out three photos of women and placed them in front of Mia. Jack recognised them as Kim, Nora and Ruth. He thought, this is too easy. There's only one young woman.

'Was the woman any of these?'

Mia screwed up her face. 'She wasn't either of those older women. Could've been this younger one. But it was dark and she wore a woolly hat.'

'Let's try for the man then.'

DS Martin laid out three photos, which Jack knew as Saul, David and Keith.

Mia blew out her cheeks and shook her head. 'He had a hat on, you know, one of those high, old fashioned ones. He could have been any of these.' She looked up at DS Martin. 'I'm not much good at recognising people. And it was dark. Just a bit of torchlight at one point. But Chitra said she knew them both.' She banged a finger on the table. 'I remember now. Chitra said the woman was the flower woman.'

DS Martin and the constable looked at each other.

'Thank you, Mia. That's most useful. Do you know where Chitra lives?'

'No, I don't.'

'Have you got a phone number?'

'I have.' Mia took out her phone, scrolled down and gave the number.

'Thank you, Mia. You have been extremely helpful. We'll see if we can locate Chitra.'

Chapter 39

Hayley and Fayyad rushed back from the cemetery to Forest Gate police station, to make the major incident meeting. They needn't have rushed, as their boss was held up in an interview. There were about a dozen men and women in the room, most of whom Fayyad recognised. There were gruesome pictures of the victim on the display boards along with various scraps of paper, which Fayyad should peruse but he wasn't going to now. They could all be called up on the large central computer screen, but DS Martin liked to have much of it visible to display the full picture to everyone as the investigation proceeded.

Hayley went off to the canteen to get them tea. They'd been working non-stop. There would be a late night tonight; they had yet to find time to write up the interviews. Everything tumbled on you at the start of an investigation. Interview on interview, which all had to be written up. He and Hayley had already had preliminary interviews with Jack, Keith and Saul. Paperwork, paperwork, the bane of their lives.

Hayley returned with a small tray holding three cups of tea. Why three, Fayyad was about to ask when DS Martin entered, and Hayley rushed over and gave her a cup. He smiled as he sipped his tea. Hayley was smart: give the boss a cup of tea and she'll remember you. Little things. Hayley was angling for promotion.

DS Nikki Martin sat on the edge of a desk, facing everyone, her tea beside her. She called everyone to order, and the chatter stopped.

'Hello, everyone,' she began. 'I'm DS Martin, as most of you know, in charge of the investigation into Kim Frank's death. This is now our major incident room. All our meetings will be held here. Most of you know each other, but there's a few I don't know. So I'd like to go round the room, for each of you to give your name, rank and unit.'

As this went on, Fayyad noted the boss giving a smile or nod as each in turn identified themselves. He jotted down a couple of names he didn't know, who might prove useful.

'Thank you, everyone,' said DS Martin, once the introductions were over. 'Most of you know the rough details. Please familiarise yourself with what goes up on these boards. Give yourself ten minutes before the meetings to get up to date. Or we are simply treading on each other's toes and repeating what other members of the team have done already. Let's get going. In short, Kim Frank was stabbed last night in Forest Gate cemetery somewhere between two and four in the morning. On the board, you'll see the location and pictures of the corpse.'

'We have a number of suspects.' She consulted her notes. 'We have Jack Bell, a builder, the last known person to see her alive. There's Keith Frank, her brother in law, known to have threatened her. Her mother, Nora Maxwell, known to have quarrelled with her too. Her uncle, David Coe, her aunt, Ruth Little, also in quarrelsome mode, and Saul Coe, her uncle. You might have noted a lot of family here and a lot of rows. They own 60% of the cemetery between them. Fayyad,' she looked over to him. 'You have the latest info on Saul Coe, our prime suspect.'

'Yes, ma'am. Saul is downstairs waiting to be interviewed. He was seen driving, not far from the cemetery, at about two thirty. Admittedly by Jack Bell. But in my opinion, Jack is a low level suspect. He was out searching for his daughter...'

'We'll come to that,' said DS Martin. 'Go on with Saul Coe.'

'He was driving near the cemetery as I've said. He says he hadn't been in there, he was just driving around as he couldn't sleep. He went as far as Epping, he says. But his pen was found at the site.' Fayyad took it out of his pocket, and held it up in a plastic evidence bag. 'Saul agreed it was his. Well, he could hardly have not as it's engraved with his name.' There was laughter round the room. 'When he was told it was found under the victim, he clammed up and said he wanted a solicitor. And, as I've said, he's downstairs awaiting an interview. Unfortunately, his solicitor can't get here for a couple of hours.'

'Then he can stew awhile. Never does any harm, going over past sins. Thank you, Fayyad.' She gave him a nod of approval. 'I've been interviewing Mia Bell, Jack Bell's daughter. She was in the cemetery last night. A dare, she says, a picnic.' More laughter. 'Well you may laugh. Teenagers these days, picnics in cemeteries after midnight. But to the point, she saw a man and a woman going into the office, some time after two. Mia was with another girl, Chitra Bhatti. Mia says that Chitra recognised the man and the woman. Chitra told her the woman was the flower stall woman, which would be Kim, the victim. Chitra knew the man too, but she didn't tell Mia who he was. Clearly, he could be the murderer. Which would eliminate Jack Bell, as his daughter would have recognised him. I agree with Fayyad, Jack slips down our list. Not quite off it. It's imperative, though, we find Chitra as soon as possible. She's an important witness. Her life could be in danger.'

Chapter 40

Alison was looking up at the ceiling, specifically at the large square cut out of the plaster board.

'How long have we got to live with that?'

She, Mia and Jack were drinking tea at the kitchen table. Alison had bought a walnut cake. She was in a light blue, worsted dress suit with a darker blue blouse. She'd put the matching jacket over the back of her chair.

'A couple of weeks,' said Jack. 'It's not worth rushing things. Let the damp dry out, or you'll only have problems later. The ceiling could stain or you might get dry rot.'

'Point taken,' she said. 'It's neatly done, even if we have to view the joists for a while. And there's no mess.'

'Don't sound so surprised.'

'A pleasant surprise,' she said, with a short laugh. 'That's why I've bought cake. Though you haven't left me an invoice.'

'I've been so rushed,' said Jack.

'He knew the murdered woman,' said Mia eagerly.

'Did you?'

He nodded.

'He went out with her,' said Mia.

'Curiouser and curiouser.' She turned to Mia. 'How was your interview?'

'The police woman said I was very helpful,' she said, before screwing up her face. 'Then I had to wait for ages while Dad made a statement. I was in this small room waiting for him, years and years. A police woman got me some tea and cake.'

'So this is your second lot. You won't eat your dinner.' She turned to Jack. 'Talking of cake, I was looking for my big knife to cut the walnut cake. You haven't seen it? Part of that set.' She indicated the wooden knife-holder on the windowsill over the sink, one compartment empty.

Jack had a thought where it was. Should he say?

'I might've used it yesterday,' he said carefully, 'when I came in to shut the water off. It was the middle of the school run, I couldn't park anywhere near the house. So I came in with only a few tools.' A few was better than admitting he'd brought none. 'And had to open that trap door by the front door to get to the stopcock. I used a meat skewer and a knife...'

'Yuk,' exclaimed Alison. 'We eat with those.'

'I put them in the dishwasher afterwards,' he said.

'Even so, Jack.'

'I could've have left the water running through your ceiling.'

'Emergency,' she said with a nod. 'OK. I'll allow it. So where's the knife?'

'I might have left it by the stopcock. I'll take a look.'

He left them. Alison waited until he was well out of the room.

She said quietly, 'You said your father was going out with the dead woman?'

'Only once,' said Mia. 'Last night, in fact.'

'I bet he was with her when I phoned about you,' she said thoughtfully. 'Then he went off to look for you, and she went off and got killed.'

'That's not very nice,' exclaimed Mia.

'You're right. Sorry. But your dad does get into some scrapes.'

'Chitra recognised the woman at the cemetery.'

'What, the corpse!'

'No. She was alive then and with a man, late last night when we were there. They were going in the office. The man was probably the killer.'

'And you were there, in the cemetery, along with a killer!'

'We didn't know.'

Jack returned.

'No knife there. What's all the fuss?'

'Your daughter tells me, she and Chitra saw the killer last night.'

'Possible killer.'

'That doesn't make me feel any better,' exclaimed Alison. She shook her head. 'I really don't know sometimes.' She turned to Jack. 'You went out with the murdered woman, Mia sees her at the cemetery.' She shook her head. 'I don't know what to make of it. You could both be arrested. Dear oh dear.' She looked at her watch. 'And I've got to be elsewhere. I've a governors' meeting. Can you stay, Jack? There's plenty of food.'

'Sure. What time will you be back?'

'About nine.' She took a deep breath and glanced at her daughter. 'Make sure Mia stays in tonight. No cemetery visits, please. Lock her in the cellar if need be.'

Chapter 41

Jack had his evening meal with Mia, a pizza and some salad. Alison returned about nine and he'd left, quite relieved to be out of Alison's ken; she could be somewhat accusatory. Back home, he had a shower. As the water ran he couldn't overcome the feeling that if he hadn't gone out looking for Mia then Kim would be alive. The two of them together through the night, and all would be well.

Less than 24 hours ago, she'd been at his table, making a will. They'd delivered a copy to Keith. What had happened to the other two copies? If Keith had torn up his copy, and if the other copies were lost, then, as Kim was still married, the house would go to her husband. And Keith could stay on forever.

So what? It had nothing to do with him where Keith lived. Kim hadn't wanted him there as she'd wanted to sell the house, but Kim was dead. The house would go to someone or other, dogs' home or a relative. What did it matter to him? Except it niggled. The house and will could be important in finding the killer.

He dressed after the shower. It was too early to go to bed and he was a little depressed and irritated that he couldn't connect anything. He'd talk to Fayyad in the morning. Maybe the cops had the will after all.

His bell rang. He wasn't expecting anyone, though it could be Fayyad with thoughts of his own. He went down the stairs and opened the front door.

It was Maria, in her tam-o'-shanter and fiery red coat. The red always turned him on, and she knew it.

'I saw your light on,' she said with a smile. 'And wondered whether you were free.'

'No,' he said, half out of fear, half out of gloom and mourning.

'Have you got someone with you?'

'Yes.' Which was true in a way.

'Do I know her?' And then she put a finger up to stop herself. 'I'm assuming a her?'

'It's a her,' he said, adding rapidly, 'You don't know her. She's setting up a coffee shop-cum-art gallery.'

'Locally?'

'She's thinking of Hackney.'

He wanted to correct himself and say, she's dead, come up and comfort me. But it was too late to backtrack. It would reveal his lie, his need.

'Some other time,' she said. And stepped forward to kiss him on the cheek in a waft of perfume and softness. With effort, he kept his arms to his side.

'Yes. Some other time,' he said. 'I'd best get back up.'

She was going down the path as he closed the door on her. Who would she visit now? Her new squeeze. But then why come here? What did it matter? Jack leaned against the closed door. He hadn't betrayed Kim's memory. He had been true. To what? To whom? Kim was dead. He'd hardly known her. Move on, move on!

He opened the front door and strode down the path, and out onto the pavement. He looked down the street, along the line of trees, the thinning leaves lit up in the yellow of the street lamps. There was Maria, maybe fifty yards away, diminished, no perfume, less red.

He watched her shrink.

Chapter 42

Saul was with his lawyer in an interview room. Opposite him were DS Nikki Martin and Fayyad. The room was windowless. A video camera was high in one corner, focused on Saul and his lawyer, showing his interviewers from an angle at the back, catching the side of their heads.

'Your solicitor says you have something to say,' said DS Martin.

Saul looked to his solicitor, Mr Greene, who nodded. Greene was almost bald, a reef of white hair around his skull. He wore a navy-blue, pin-striped suit and had an old fashioned briefcase at his feet. Fayyad could see he fitted with Saul, both of the same type. They'd had a long chat before the interview, exasperating Fayyad and his boss who'd wanted to get the session over with and go home.

'Yes, I want to correct something,' said Saul. He took another glance at his solicitor, a deep breath. 'This is all being recorded?'

'It is.'

'Then for the record, I was driving away from the cemetery last night.'

'Earlier, you told my colleague, Detective Sergeant Fayyad Kamani, you didn't go there.'

'I take that back,' said Saul. 'It was stupid of me to say it.'

'It never helps,' said DS Martin. 'But you were there. Why?'

'I drove there to meet my niece, Kim.'

'What time was this?'

'I arrived at two thirty.'

'That's rather late for a rendezvous, wouldn't you say?'

'I had to give her some money.' He shifted uncomfortably in his collar and looked at Greene who nodded. 'It was a private arrangement. I didn't want anyone else knowing.'

'You mean your family?'

'Yes.' He took a sip of water. 'The time suited me. I don't sleep well. Kim phoned me a little while before. She knows – she knew I'm often awake in the early hours.'

'What did she want?'

'She said she needed the cash I'd promised her. Daytime, as I've said, wasn't convenient. She was awake, I was awake. Let's get it done with, I told her.'

'How much did you give her?'

'Ten thousand pounds.'

'You keep that much in your safe?'

'It's a strong safe. There are times I need cash.'

'I suspect some sly dealing, Mr Coe, but my business is murder, not tax evasion. Tell me what happened at the cemetery.'

'I drove there. She'd walked there and was already at the gate when I arrived. We went into the office. I opened the safe and I gave her the money. While she was counting it, I got a phone call. My wife Sarah was having a fit. Her carer, Badrah, phoned to tell me. Sarah has a number of carers to cover the week. Badrah had called an ambulance. I drove home immediately.'

'Leaving Kim?'

'She was in the office. She had a key to the cemetery. I left her counting the money. How was I to know what would happen?'

'That was the last you saw of her?'

'I'm afraid so.' He sighed and wiped his brow. 'I should have given her a lift. But she insisted she'd be fine. She told me to look after Sarah.' He stopped. 'It was a false alarm anyway. I sent the ambulance away. You can check on that.'

He showed his open hands in incomprehension. 'How was I to know what would happen to Kim?'

'A word, if I may,' said Mr Greene.

'By all means.'

Greene spoke slowly and formally. 'My client wishes to apologise for holding back this information. He thought it might put him in a bad light. It could be easily misconstrued. I advised him to tell the truth; it would only come out if he didn't.'

'Quite right, Mr Greene. That is, if your client is now telling the truth.' She turned to Saul. 'I am afraid I'm not altogether convinced by your tale. I accept you went to the cemetery, I accept you met your niece. What happened after that, I shall need more persuading before I accept your version. That being the case, you are going to be kept in custody tonight. In the morning, we'll continue with this interview.'

Chapter 43

Next morning, Jack rose late, with little enthusiasm. He hadn't put the alarm on as he had no work, his site being a crime scene. Once upright, he searched the kitchen for remnants of food, finding a small lump of cheese, an egg and a crust of bread. It would have to do. Today, he had no excuse not to go shopping.

While eating he reflected on Maria's visit. It had depressed him. Some people are able to come and go sexually, have open relationships, friendship and a roll. He couldn't do it, even if he'd wanted to, which he admitted might be worth a try, but only if he were someone else. He'd be too jealous, too wound up.

He was bad at managing stress. Avoid it, said Alcohol Halt, his local recovery group. Such advice is easy to give, but self employment is stressful by its nature, with difficult customers, suppliers, the weather, an item on the job not accounted for, chasing payment. Not forgetting the bank and the mortgage, or Alison, and his various relationships, mostly short lived. He was doing it again, the very thing he shouldn't, making a list of the kicks in store. No wonder he could hardly get up.

Avoid stress. Stop complaining.

Post breakfast, he washed the dishes. All of them. What good habits he was developing. Look on the bright side. More AH advice. And to counteract it, he looked at his bank account online. Not quite as bad as it might be. At least he was in the black, but the mortgage was due in a week or two. He must get some leaflets printed and post them through letterboxes. Always the way with work, either too much or twiddling your thumbs.

He put his dirty washing in the machine, went out and did some shopping while the machine chugged, feeling better now he was on the move. The sky was clear, he noted; he could get out with his telescope tonight. That always cheered him up. The immensity of the universe versus our petty concerns. Back home, he flicked through his astronomy magazine to this month's night sky pages. There was a half moon tonight, Jupiter in the east about nine, Mars around too. And he might catch some shooting stars.

So he'd be out. Cross fingers for clear skies and take the scope to Wanstead Flats. He used to go out to Epping Forest, but that was a chore of a drive. By the time he got there, the sky had often clouded over. At least Wanstead Flats was only a few minutes away.

It was a little past noon when Jack drove to the cemetery. He parked outside the gates. No tools needed as he wouldn't be working. He went in, unencumbered. Just up the way, he saw Ruth with a small watering can at the flower stall.

'They're still up there, Jack,' she said as he approached. 'All that criss-cross tape. Heaven knows what they're looking for.'

Ruth was over made up as usual, too much perfume, or was it her hair lacquer? She wore an orange dress with a red jumper; the colour effecting no passion in Jack. There were red highlights in her blonde hair, causing Jack to wonder how early she rose to get herself ready for the world.

'They're looking for traces,' he said. 'A footprint, a cigarette butt, a bus ticket.' He'd talked it over a few months back with Fayyad when he'd gone to visit him and his family in Ilford. Murderers in haste leave vestiges of themselves.

'They questioned me for over an hour,' she exclaimed, all flailing hands. 'Wanted to know what I was doing at two thirty in the morning.' She laughed. 'What did they think I was doing? In the arms of my toy boy? Chance would be a fine thing. I was fast asleep, on my own, the only witness my cat, Biggles, asleep at my feet.'

'I thought I'd take a look at the site,' said Jack. 'Ask them how long they're likely to be.'

An elderly man was holding out a bunch of chrysanthemums for attention. Ruth went off to deal with him, and Jack left her, proceeding towards the crematorium. At least today he wouldn't find a corpse. If there was one, a cop would have found it. Did they leave a guard overnight?

Cars were parked outside the crematorium, flowers against the wall, a wreath saying DAD. He could just hear the strains of *We Will Rock You* from inside, and wondered about Dad, an old rocker perhaps, to be buried along with his electric guitar.

Conkers and brown rolled leaves lay on the tarmac on the side road. A squirrel clambered up a tree as he came close. Jack picked up a conker and would have thrown it, but recalled his annoyance at Mia, and put it in his pocket. Why this primitive urge to throw things? Didn't the poor animal have enough problems with winter coming, without a brute human using it for pot-shots?

His pile of bricks was at the limit of the police tape. It surrounded his site, in a square with sides around 50 yards long. There were three figures inside, of indeterminate sex, in baggy white coveralls, head to foot. There was a small marquee over the patch where he'd found the body. His plastic sheet was poking out from underneath. He wondered how much mess the investigators were making, though he might be OK. It was their job to be careful, not in any consideration for him, but not to disturb the ground.

A police officer in uniform was standing just within the boundary. Jack beckoned, and the officer strolled over.

'I was working here, officer,' said Jack, taking care to be polite. 'You wouldn't know how much longer they're likely to be?'

The police constable's tongue lolled in his cheek. His thinking mode. 'Be done with later today from what I've heard. With luck, you could get back tomorrow.'

'That's good news,' he said. 'I'm a mate of Fayyad Kamani. Do you know him?'

Definitely the right question. The police officer beamed. 'I'm in the police cricket team with him. He's our number one batsman. Last match of the season this Saturday.'

'We were at school together in Plaistow,' said Jack. 'Keep bumping into each other. I'm a builder, I get around, he's a cop, gets about too. I know his boss likes him.'

'She's OK.' He laughed. 'A cricket umpire, so anyone in the team is in her good books. She likes Fayyad. Who doesn't? They're on this case.' He leaned in closer. 'Family affair, this one. One of the brothers, they reckon. Keep it to yourself.'

'Sure,' said Jack, that assessment being more or less what he thought. Saul perhaps. David less likely.

He thanked him and wandered off, not quite sure where to go. And returned to a thought he'd had last night. Chitra. Driving around looking for them, he'd thought that she could be sleeping in the cemetery. It was what had drawn him here last night, where he'd found the two girls climbing over the fence.

So she might be basing herself somewhere in here. And she needed to be found. She was a valuable witness. Her life could be in danger. Half an hour wandering about would do him no harm. He'd nothing better to do. Where to start? He needed to get into her head. What did Chitra want? A safe place to sleep, somewhere to keep her gear. She'd need some sort of shelter and privacy. A tent was unlikely, a chore to put up every night. Besides, it would have to be hidden during the day, along with her possessions. When Jack had caught her at Alison's, all she'd had was a backpack.

As he ambled, he couldn't help reading the gravestones. It struck him again how everyone was sadly missed, beloved by wife and family, 'a light from the hearth has gone', 'never an unkindly word', dear husband, darling wife. Where were the wife beaters buried, the miserable uncle or aunt, the bullying mother, incestuous father and nasty kids? Dead, you get the family blessing.

Here and there were small, white military gravestones from the First and Second World War. A neat parade of them, near the railway fence. Young men, from army, air force, and navy; sad memorials for lives cut short. So many.

Some tombs had epitaphs in rhyme. Alison had said she'd never seen a good verse in a graveyard. It was as if we returned to childhood for our last jingle.

Beyond these distractions, he couldn't find anything where one might shelter overnight. He looked along the railway fence, perhaps a gap. And encountered bindweed and ivy, but nowhere to hide or get through to the cutting above the railway line.

He was held by the family grave of the Deaths. What a name! A large tombstone, dating back to late Victorian times. It must surely be pronounced De-ath, he thought. Though death was its tale. A saga of infant mortality: dead babies, young children, a girl who had got to the ripe old age of seventeen, while Mother and Father Death lived on to see them all pass away. Not so long ago, a hundred or so years. Before the age of mass vaccinations and antibiotics, making Jack grateful he was alive now, instead of the disease-wracked past.

He strayed into patches of woodland. Perhaps amongst the bushes and trees, she might take shelter, a hollow tree. One patch had woodland graves, signified not with grave-stones but small plaques on the trees, with faded flowers shrivelled at the trunks. Trees would give some protection from the weather, but where would she leave her possessions? Mourners came here, and graveyard staff. Mr Coe would spot anything out of place.

The lines of new graves, he rejected. Too uniform, the ranks of them with space between to run a tractor mower. No hiding place there. He ambled round the perimeter, by the fence, pushing through brambles and nettles. There were houses on three sides, the other had the railway cutting. Could she have climbed into one of these gardens, made an abandoned shed her own? Risky. How would you know a shed was abandoned?

Where would she go, a girl who'd run away from home, afraid she'd be sent back, if caught, by the authorities? Or put into foster care. That's if she didn't end up in jail for burglary. Though a judge might show clemency, as Jack had. But what to do with her? Where could such a girl be placed where she wouldn't abscond?

She was an outlaw. At least, until she was an adult and could work. If she chose to. In the meantime, she had to have a safe shelter and a way of obtaining money to keep going.

He came across the mausoleum, a little way up from the flower stall. He had considered it earlier but rejected it for its grimness. Made from stone, with no windows, presumably coffins on shelves inside. Who would choose to sleep in there?

Someone desperate. Who valued safety above all else.

It was the only mausoleum in the cemetery. There were family graves, but this was the only one with a house-like structure. Would anyone really bed down in there? He realised, he wasn't putting himself in her shoes. He, himself, would most certainly reject the stone chamber, but she was a young and vulnerable girl. Perhaps she'd been pestered on the streets.

He walked round the small building. It was well built, gothic, like a mini church, the size of a small room. He examined the door; he'd have to bend his head to go inside. Just wide enough for a coffin. And he noted the hinges had been oiled. Quite recently. There were scratches round the lock, where someone had tried to fit in the key, perhaps in the dark. Jack got down to his knees. There was a faint arc scratched in the dust where the door would open.

He phoned Fayyad.

PART FOUR:
IN THE MAUSOLEUM

Chapter 44

While waiting, Jack went into the office. Maureen rose from her small desk and came to the counter. She was attractive in a white blouse and blue skirt. A full figure. But married, he recalled. Not everyone was waiting for him.

'You'll be relieved to know,' she said with a smile, 'the boss isn't in.'

'Thank heaven for that,' exclaimed Jack. 'Where is he? Fallen off a cliff, by any stroke of luck?'

'I don't know,' she said with a shrug. 'He phoned first thing. Just said he wouldn't be in. Didn't say why or where he was. Might be his wife Sarah, might be a business meeting. I don't know. He does that from time to time. He told me to hold the fort.'

'I'm sure you do that very well,' said Jack. 'And I'm wondering if you can help me.' He pointed out of the window. 'That mausoleum, there. What do you know about it?'

'Not much,' she said, gazing in its direction, 'beyond the fact it's been there a long time. Late Victorian, isn't it? Not been in use for well over a hundred years.'

'There wouldn't be a key, would there?'

'Why?'

'I have the feeling someone has been in there in the last few days. The hinges are oiled, there's recent scratching round the key hole...'

'I don't know of any key,' she said. 'But then, why would I? I would think no one has asked for it since before the First World War. What's the name of the family?'

'Baron,' he said. 'There's a couple of Henry Barons and a Mathilda Baron.'

Maureen went to the back shelving. From a wide shelf of old journals, she took down a large, fat tome. It was weighty and she carried it with both arms to the counter.

'This one runs from the mid 1880s to the early 1900s. We get researchers sometimes from the universities wanting to see it. Researching child mortality, also genealogy is popular these days, people tracing family histories.'

She flicked through the book. There were rows upon rows, written in brown ink in a copperplate hand.

'Can you give me an exact year?' she said.

'Henry Baron died in 1896,' he said. 'He was the last of them I found on the plaques.'

'Baron, Baron,' she said, as she travelled down the columns with a finger, turning pages. 'A lot of deaths in those days. Plenty of children. Women in childbirth...'

'You seem knowledgeable,' he said.

'I've an MA in local history,' she said, as she continued her search. 'I like cemeteries. Lots of people don't, but I'm fascinated by old gravestones. They tell us who we were, or really, who we are. There's more than just bones in a grave-yard.' She stabbed a finger. 'Ah! Here we are. Henry Baron. Got him. In the family mausoleum, yes, yes.' She looked up. 'And there is a key. That's a surprise. And we are the holder.'

'Remarkable,' said Jack. 'Can you find it?'

'We have a key rack,' she said. 'There aren't many keys there. That's our only mausoleum. Let's have a look.'

She went to the side wall, where there was a squarish, flat box screwed to the wall, the size of a tabloid newspaper. From a drawer nearby, she took out a bunch of keys. Searching the bunch, she found the one she wanted and opened the rack door. Inside were rows of labelled hooks with keys dangling from them. She perused them, going along rows. Then for a second time.

'It's missing,' she said. She indicated an empty hook. 'There, under the hook, it says Baron mausoleum. Gone.' She opened her hands to show her ignorance. 'No idea when. Could have been yesterday, could have been a hundred and twenty years ago.'

'I think yesterday is closer,' said Jack.

He turned around on hearing the door. Fayyad had entered. Immaculate as always in his suit, white shirt and tie. How did he stay so tidy?

'So, Jack,' said Fayyad with a mock frown, 'what have you to tell me that's so important? You know I hate to be interrupted when I'm writing up reports.' He dropped his frown. 'Actually, anything is relief from paperwork. Just to stretch my legs and get outside is a blessing.'

'Would you gentlemen like a cup of tea?' asked Maureen.

'Love one, Maureen,' said Jack. 'Oh, isn't this place pleasant without Mr Coe!'

'We're holding him for questioning,' said Fayyad.

'I wondered where he was,' said Maureen. 'He was even more secretive than he usually is when he phoned me earlier. Did you say you wanted tea, sergeant?'

'Yes, please, Maureen.' He turned back to Jack. 'What have you got to show me, Jack, that's so epoch-making?'

'You still looking for Chitra?'

'We most certainly are. We believe she's at risk. Her phone is constantly off which is worrying. Her parents have had no contact with her for over a year. Why? Do you know where she is?'

'I think so.'

Chapter 45

They went out to the mausoleum. Jack told Fayyad his thoughts about Chitra: how he'd found her stealing at Alison's, how little she'd had with her. And his guess that she could be sleeping somewhere in the cemetery that had led him to finding the girls the night before last.

Jack showed Fayyad the oiled hinges, the scratches round the keyhole, the arc in the dust.

'Someone's been in there,' mused Fayyad. 'But it doesn't have to be Chitra.'

'I did find the girls climbing over the gate. And Chitra can pick locks. I bet she got the key out of the office key rack.'

'She won't be in there now,' said Fayyad.

'Not likely,' said Jack. 'Probably comes back when the cemetery is shut.'

'Let's have a think before we go charging in,' said Fayyad, strolling round the stone building. 'I don't want to look a prize idiot. But then again, I might be a bigger idiot not breaking in.'

'Any damage, I can repair,' said Jack. 'Might there be a budget for that sort of thing?'

'If we find something important, most definitely. I'll get a round of applause at the incident meeting and the boss will gladly pay up. If we find nothing, she'll be a right grouch.'

'More work on spec,' said Jack. 'Typical. But I'm not doing anything else. Your gang is all over my site. Shall we go in?'

'Let's not be too hasty.' He was scratching his cheek. 'Let's suppose that Chitra's not in there now. But her things are. What we'd need to do is get inside, then wait for her to come back.'

Jack nodded. 'I see where you're heading. She won't go in if the door's damaged.'

'She'll take one look and run for it. And that'll be the last we see of her.'

Jack looked at the door, then the stonework of the walls. 'I could take out some stone blocks at the back,' he said. 'When you go in to wait for her, the stones could be put back in without the mortar.'

Fayyad shuddered. 'Be like being buried alive. There's corpses there.'

Jack laughed. 'Bring a big torch. Think of it, if you find Chitra they'll put your name in lights.'

'Not if I go screaming off in the middle of the night... They'd never let me forget it.'

'You need company. Who's that mate of yours? That tall woman.'

'Hayley, yeh. I'm sure she could scare off a zombie or two. Let's get in.'

Jack went off to collect his tools from his van. In a cloth bag, he put two cold chisels, a club hammer, goggles, leather gloves and a brush. And a torch, of course, for when they were inside. What else? He shrugged. If he needed anything else, the van was only a short walk away. In fact, he could have driven it in with no Coe about. And with police permission too.

Never mind.

Returning, he saw Maureen coming across from the office balancing a tray with two mugs of tea, heading for Fayyad who was waiting by the mausoleum.

'What are you going to do here?' she said cautiously, handing them their mugs of tea.

'Breaking in,' said Fayyad.

'Oh no, you can't do that,' she exclaimed. 'Mr Coe'll go mad.'

'Your boss is in custody,' said Fayyad. 'I could get a search warrant of course. That's a nuisance as I'm here now.

But I would get one. On the other hand, there could be the body of a young girl in there.'

You don't believe that, thought Jack. Though it was not impossible.

'Or she could be badly injured,' went on Fayyad, 'and time is of the essence.'

'I could get in the most awful trouble,' she said, her hand going to her cheek.

'This is a murder enquiry,' insisted Fayyad.

'I'll make good any damage,' added Jack. 'It'll be better than new.'

She gave him a smile, welcoming his thoughtfulness.

'Do it,' she said. 'Just back me up, please.'

'Promise,' said Fayyad.

She left them. Jack hoped he was right and Chitra was using the place. He didn't want Maureen bawled out by Coe. If this was Chitra's lair then there'd be no hassle. If it wasn't, there could be a dressing down all round.

He put on the goggles and gloves and set to work at the back of the mausoleum. Having decided to go for stones at the base, he began by chipping out mortar around a large square stone. Once the first was out, it should be easy enough to remove a few more.

The mortar was soft and old. It had never been re-pointed. He had the first block out in five minutes, two more out in ten.

'Done,' said Jack. 'Just a quick clean up and in we go.'

The gap was at ground level and dusty. With the brush, Jack swept away the mortar dust and chippings.

'Who's first?' said Jack.

'It'll ruin my suit,' complained Fayyad.

'Why don't you ask Maureen if she's got some overalls?'

'Good idea.' And Fayyad was off.

Jack knelt down to peer into the gap. He shone his torch about, playing it around the space. He could make out the door across the other side, shelves on the sides. The floor was tidy with no sign of a body, which was a relief. Would they find anything else?

Fayyad came out of the office wearing a brown warehouse coat. He smiled, indicating his new attire.

'Maureen won't get into trouble, Jack,' he said. 'I just remembered, Saul Coe is into some tax fiddle. He keeps too much cash in his safe. I'll remind him of that, should he think of having a go at her.'

Jack grinned. Fayyad was too thoughtful to be a cop.

'I'll go in first,' he said. He wasn't worried about his clothes, wearing everyday jeans and a sweatshirt.

He got down on his back and eased himself in head first. Once inside, his feet sticking out of the gap, there was sufficient light for him to see shelves on either side. As his eyes adjusted, he saw three coffins, one of the lower shelves being empty. But it was altogether too clean. There should be a century or more of dust in here. Someone was using the place. There was a faint smell, he sniffed, incense perhaps, or the sort of scented candle that Alison used.

And yes, there was a candle stub on a shelf recessed into the back wall, alongside an urn.

'Pass me the torch, Fayyad.'

Fayyad handed it through. 'I'm coming in,' he said. 'Give me lots of light.'

Jack turned on the torch as Fayyad crawled in on his stomach. Jack moved back and stood up to give him room, his head a few inches from the roof.

'Not as bad as I thought,' said Fayyad, rising to his feet and brushing himself down. 'Though I wouldn't like to be here at night.'

'You might yet have to be,' said Jack, showing him the candle.

It was when they brought down the urn that they found the money and necklace in the recess.

Chapter 46

The necklace went into an evidence bag. Jack recognised it as the one Kim had been wearing the last time he'd seen her. The money was in a canvas bag, in bundles of notes each held together by an elastic band. Tentatively, Jack had opened a lower coffin, expecting a skeleton, but in fact found a dress, jeans, underwear, a sleeping bag, make-up, a towel, soap, toothpaste and a letter from a homeless charity to Chitra Bhatti.

They'd found her.

Fayyad said they should leave the items in the coffin except the letter. He put the necklace and the letter, both bagged, into his pocket, and they crawled out of the mauso-leum with the canvas bag of money. They went to Fayyad's car, which was parked just up from the office. From the boot, Fayyad removed gloves and a plastic sheet.

'We need to keep everything clean,' he said. 'This is evid-ence.'

They went into the office. Maureen was at her station typing. She looked up as they entered.

Fayyad said, 'We want to use Coe's office. Just for a short while.'

'I can hardly stop you,' she said. 'Please leave it tidy.'

'He won't know we've been there,' said Fayyad.

'Did you find what you were looking for?'

'We did,' said Jack. 'A girl's been staying in the mauso-leum for some while.'

'Who'd have guessed that?'

'No one will say anything about you giving us permission to break in,' said Fayyad.

'I didn't exactly give you permission,' she said.

'We've only taken out a few blocks,' added Jack. 'I'll cement them in tomorrow.'

'Too much excitement for me,' she said flapping her hands. 'Nothing ever happens here.'

Fayyad and Jack went into Saul's office. The plastic sheet was placed on his desk. Fayyad, wearing gloves, emptied the money from the canvas bag onto the sheet. He counted one of the bundles of notes. It was in 20s, five hundred pounds in all. There were nineteen similarly sized bundles and one smaller packet.

After totting up on a piece of scrap paper, Fayyad said, '£9,900 in total. This has to be the cash that Coe gave to Kim.'

Seeing Jack's expression, he realised Jack knew nothing of the transaction. And so Fayyad put him in the picture, telling him what Coe had admitted at the interview last night. How Coe had come here to meet Kim and had given her ten thousand pounds. Then left her to get back to his ailing wife.

'Do you believe he simply left Kim here?' asked Jack.

'It's rather convenient, that phone call,' admitted Fayyad. 'We're questioning his wife's carer this afternoon, and contacting the ambulance service about the time of the call to them. But whatever they say, times are imprecise. And it would have taken no time at all to stab Kim.'

'But why do it at my site?' He was staring at the pile of bank notes. 'All that cash. If Saul Coe had killed Kim, he wouldn't leave her with it.'

'And what is Chitra doing with it?'

'Stole it somehow,' mused Jack. He stopped, unable to complete the thought.

Fayyad shrugged. 'We have to question her. Find out how she got the money. Though it does prove Coe was telling the truth when he said he took the cash out of his safe. Close to ten thou there, so it's likely Chitra's taken a hundred as pocket money and left the rest in the bag for later.'

'The girl's a thief. She'll take anything not chained down. And maybe the chain too, if she can pick the lock.'

'She's a vital witness,' said Fayyad. 'We've got to catch her, before someone else does.'

Fayyad began putting the money back into the canvas bag.

'A good afternoon's work, Jack. I owe you one. But first things first: I've got to take the swag to the police station. I'll come back here with Hayley tonight to wait for Chitra in the mausoleum.' He shuddered. 'I'm not looking forward to that. Creepy place. I'm not superstitious, but a mausoleum at night is not my favourite bolt hole.' He waved a hand in dismissal of his fears. 'All in the line of duty. We have to catch her, for her own sake. We need to know how she got the cash and who she saw that night. I'd be grateful if you can put the stones back in the gap, loosely, no mortar, so we can get them out easily when we come back tonight.'

'No problem.'

Once Fayyad had filled the canvas bag with the money, he put it into a large evidence sack, bag and all. And then left with the new findings: the money, bracelet and the letter. Jack was gratified that they'd located Chitra. The girl might be a thief but needed protection. And he'd got work from the cops out of it. How much might he invoice them? It wouldn't do to take liberties, but £120 or so would probably pass. After all, it was his brainwork and search that had traced Chitra.

Useful cash to tide him over. And with luck, he'd be back on site tomorrow.

Jack thanked Maureen for her help, informing her the boss' office was spick and span. He'd go over now to tidy up at the mausoleum, and would be back tomorrow to do the final repairs.

He left her.

Behind the mausoleum, Jack collected the scraps of old mortar in a bucket, and brushed away any remaining dust and chippings. He was putting the stones back in the gap, when his phone rang. An unknown number.

'Jack of All Trades?' asked a woman.

'That's me,' said Jack. 'What can I do for you?'

'I'm locked out. Can you help? I'm on Capel Road by the Flats.'

Chapter 47

It was only a few minutes' drive to Capel Road. The road ran along the north end of Wanstead Flats, with houses on one side and the Flats on the other. Football pitches were at this end, half hidden by trees, easing away to bumpier grass-land and copses of trees and shrubs.

The young woman was sitting on her step. She was small and slim, her elbows on her knees, obviously unhappy.

'I closed the door,' she exclaimed, 'and instantly knew I'd locked my keys inside. They're on the kitchen table; I can see them grinning at me.'

'Keys do that,' he said.

Jack was looking at the house. It was large, a Victorian house, two storeys.

'You have neighbours in the house?' he said.

She flapped a hand to show there was no help there. 'They're in Thailand for the next two weeks.'

'And you don't fancy sitting on the step waiting.'

'No.' She didn't find the comment funny.

Jack examined the front door. It was solid, possibly oak. If he broke in there, he would certainly smash the door post, damage the door and make the lock unusable too.

'I don't want to go in that way,' he said, coming back to her. 'The door and fittings would cost hundreds to replace.'

'There's another locked door inside too,' she said dismally. 'A small hallway, then two doors. One for upstairs, one for me, downstairs.'

'We'll have to break a window then,' he said. 'Cheaper to replace. Now which one?'

'It's all double glazed,' she said. 'Not cheap.'

'No, it wouldn't be.' Two lots of glass to break through. Probably have to buy a new unit. 'There,' he said, looking down some steps at the outside of the house. 'Your cellar. That's not double glazed. Is it?'

'No.'

'Be a bit of a squeeze,' he said, looking at the narrow window. 'I might get stuck, but you'd be OK.'

'Break it,' she said, instantly cheering up. She stood up from the front step. 'I knew you'd be fine. Maria recommended you.'

'Did she now?' he exclaimed in some surprise.

'You poly?' she enquired, following him as he went to his van for tools.

'Poly?' he said. 'Sorry. I don't know what that is.'

'Multiple partners,' she said. 'Maria was trying to be poly.' She laughed. 'I am. But she's too possessive. It's only sex. You can't be clingy. Be like Gauguin in the South Seas, hang loose. She couldn't do it.'

'You sent her packing,' he said as he selected tools, 'about ten the other night.' He took out a club hammer, goggles, a cold chisel, gloves and a hessian sack.

'I did. How did you know?'

'She came to my place,' he said. 'But I was busy.' He hadn't been, or maybe he was, but didn't want to explain the complications.

'You poly then?'

She walked just behind him, as he went along the path and down the steps to the cellar. She sat on the top step.

'No,' he said. 'Stand back.'

She stood up and took several steps back as he smashed into the glass with the club hammer. It shattered, the shards spilling, mostly inside. He bashed out the pieces of glass sticking out of the wood, going round the frame, thinking, is this a come on? He didn't fancy her, a pity that, as she was poly. He'd picked up the lingo.

The glass out, he folded the sack in half, and placed it over the bottom of the open frame for a cushion.

'In you go,' he said.

He gave her a hoist up, and she scrambled through the window. A minute later, she was out the front door waving her keys.

Chapter 48

'There are developments,' said Detective Superintendent Martin.

She was half perched on the desk, facing her assembled team in the major incident room.

'Let's start with the knife.' She pressed the remote in her hand, and a picture of the knife in a clear plastic bag came up on the large computer screen. 'It was found on the railway cutting. Obviously the perpetrator wanted to get rid of it quickly, and wasn't thinking clearly. There's a few dried blood droplets on it as you can see, and one unidentified print.' She looked around the room, peeved as a woman police constable tried to creep in holding a plastic cup.

'If you haven't time for tea,' she said sharply, 'don't get one.'

'Sorry, ma'am,' said the woman sheepishly.

A few of the others looked at each other, glad it wasn't them.

'These meetings start on time...' she began, when in rushed Fayyad. Her hand slapped her cheek. There were a few muffled sniggers. 'You too, Fayyad?'

'Sorry, ma'am,' he said, straightening his collar. 'I had to get evidence to forensics.'

'At least you didn't go for a cup of tea.' She held up a hand as a peace gesture. 'Sorry, everyone. It was a long day yesterday for all of us. Sorry, Amanda, you deserve a cup of tea.'

The police woman smiled.

'And I know you've been busy, Fayyad. So an apology to you too.'

'Thank you, ma'am.'

There were knowing grins. Most of them knew he was a favourite. Apologies were a good sign. She wouldn't be all bark today.

'You all know the importance of the first day or two of an investigation,' she went on. 'Before memories cloud and traces get rained away. So if a few of us are a bit sharp, lacking sleep, I apologise for my crankiness. But let's get on. This appears to be a family affair. I have just interviewed David Coe, the crematorium manager. He certainly wasn't pleased with his niece, she voted for the wrong side at the meeting. At the time of murder, he was at his girlfriend's. He's married, but not happily so, he gambles – always a motive. Certainly in need of cash. He quarrelled with his girlfriend, and he left her about two in the morning. He says he went to the casino in Stratford where he spent the next two hours. We are examining CCTV footage from there. Timing is crucial. His girlfriend lives only five minutes' drive from the cemetery. So let's not rule him out. But our prime suspect is Saul Coe. He's in the custody suite right now. His story is he went to the cemetery to meet his niece, Kim. He gave her ten thousand pounds from the safe and left her there, as he got a call from his wife's carer, saying his wife was having a fit. We also know that Chitra Bhatti saw two people going into the office about two thirty, a man and a woman who we now believe to be the victim, Kim. So it seems the man was Saul Cole.' She noted Fayyad with his hand raised. 'You have something to add, Fayyad?'

'Yes, ma'am. I got a call from Jack Bell, who is an old friend of mine. He told me there were signs the mausoleum at the cemetery was being lived in. I went over and we broke in. Easily repairable, I assure you, ma'am. Inside we found money in notes and a necklace which Jack recognised as belonging to the victim. Also clothing and a letter. Addressed to Chitra Bhatti.'

There was an intake of breath around the room. Several of them had been detailed to find her.

'How much money?' asked DS Martin.

'Nine thousand nine hundred pounds. We believe it to be the money that Saul Cole gave Kim, with a hundred taken out. With your permission, ma'am, DC Amis and I will be going to the mausoleum tonight, to wait for Chitra to return.'

'You up for that, Hayley?' asked DS Martin with a wry grin.

'I'm not afraid of ghosts, ma'am.'

'Look after Fayyad, will you,' she said, 'he's more easily spooked.' A little laughter. Fayyad shifted in his collar. 'You did well, Fayyad. Chitra has been evasive. The phone number we've been given doesn't respond. We suspect she has a new phone. Her parents and her school have been no help. So this is good news. She is a vital witness, having seen two people come into the cemetery, one the victim, the other a man that she recognised. Saul Coe, we think.'

'I had to make a decision quickly, ma'am,' said Fayyad. 'I tried calling you but you were in an interview. So I okayed Jack Bell breaking into the mausoleum. I told him he'd be paid for the break in and repairs.'

'No problem,' she said. 'The two of you have saved us a lot of man-hours searching for Chitra. Up to two hundred I'll sign off. No more than that, please. Let's move on to the crime scene. Anything new to report there?'

Chapter 49

Jack was eating at Forest Café, by the window, watching the world go by. The café was cheap, a no-frills eatery, a few doors down from Forest Gate train station. He'd been paid £60 in cash on the small job by the poly woman, Beryl. He'd had glass and putty in the van, so was able to replace the window there and then. Beryl was overjoyed to get her keys back and the window repaired. He'd suggested she get another set cut and give them to someone, while she'd suggested he might come up to her flat. But he'd felt no chemistry, so said, best not as he wasn't poly. She accepted that in good grace.

Poly is as poly does.

As he ate, he considered the chemistry of attraction. Body shape obviously, face, hair, clothing, perfume. All the physical stuff. He'd said to Beryl, as he was finishing off, that he was going out on the Flats with his telescope tonight. Would she like to come? She looked at him as if he was crazy. A not uncommon response, but it had knocked further points off her sex appeal.

Looks and rapport. With such insights, he should write for a teen mag.

The street was busy, the tail end of the rush hour streaming out of the train station. Almost night, the shops bright, the streetlights on, all the vehicles lit. The light pollution of urban living. Not that he wanted to live in Victorian gloom, to be struck on the head and robbed by a footpad in a fetid street. But please, less of the blaze.

Which was why he went off to Wanstead Flats for his observing, to a spot right in the centre, as far away from lighting as he could get. Not far enough, but the best that could be done round here. The plan was a bite to eat, then collect his gear for a few hours star gazing. There was no rush. Full darkness was needed for a good night with the telescope. And clear skies, of course. Tonight was semi clear, some stars would be visible, others hidden in cloud. He'd learnt to make the best of such nights.

For his meal, Jack had a fry up, not stinting, with money in his pocket. Chips, sausages, beans and burger, plus bread and butter, and two cups of tea, one while waiting, one during the meal. A thoroughly unhealthy meal, Alison would have told him. As he sipped his second cup, he considered whether to have a sweet or not. But he was full enough, and he wouldn't enjoy the telescope session if he had extra. He beat down his sweet tooth.

Jack reflected on the day. He and Fayyad had found Chitra. Or rather, found her habitation. Fayyad and Hayley were going to be waiting for her tonight. He had sympathy for the girl, but you can't live by stealing. No one will trust you, you'll have no friends. Or the wrong ones. He'd known that feeling well enough, when his only friends had been fellow drunks. They'd buy you a drink, be happy to see you, while others crossed the street when they saw you coming their way.

He should go back to Alcohol Halt. Though it was difficult going once in a while. When he'd gone regularly, it was a pattern, he had timetabled it. Now it was a sometime thing, when he had nothing better to do. Not good.

Jack finished his tea. He left a pound coin on the table for a tip and paid up. This place had seen some changeovers. It was run by Poles these days, open before 7 am, which was fine when he had nothing in the fridge, and closed late, fine for the same reason.

The traffic was slow and impatient on the high street. A pizza motorbike joined the traffic stream as Jack made his way between semi-stationary vehicles and down Hampton Road where he'd parked. His telescope was in the back wrapped in a plastic sheet. The sky was near dark and Jack was eager to swathe himself in the universe.

Once in the van, he drove up to the high street, and turned right to drive north, straight up the road, past both railway stations, to where the housing stopped and the road cut Wanstead Flats into two halves. And then drove on for a quarter of a mile, with the Flats on both sides of the road. It amused him that some estate agents had begun calling the place Wanstead Common, as those who didn't know the area might think the Flats were an estate of apartment blocks. No, he wanted to yell, it is an old name, he'd never known it as anything else. A flat area of grassland, three or four hundred acres of football pitches and scrub, with no one there at night but the occasional runner or dog walker. And Jack, from time to time, with his scope.

He turned into the car park, halfway down the Flats. On weekends it was used by men, mostly men, with remote controlled model aircraft. Jack would watch them flying noisily around, dipping up and down, but far preferred watching kites. Quiet and majestic, rolling high in the sky. He'd always wanted a box kite and would get one. That was an old promise. He and Mia could go out together on the Flats or to West Ham Park. She'd love that. So would he. Why not this weekend, now he had a bit of spare cash? They could go together and buy a family kite.

Jack was unwrapping the plastic from the body of his telescope when it struck him. The plastic wrapping, the need for protection.

Chapter 50

Fayyad and Hayley were in the mausoleum. Beforehand, they'd debated what light to take in with them. Nothing that could be seen from outside. Something small that would last, as they could be inside for six hours or more. Not a lantern, too noisy. They settled on a small, powerful torch along with extra batteries. The slightest sound, they would switch off instantly. The two of them sat in semi-darkness in folding director's chairs. They had brought with them water, chocolate, and energy bars. They'd reluctantly rejected coffee; the smell would give them away, ditto oranges or any hot food.

They'd come in during twilight. Fayyad had parked on a side street away from the cemetery. Chitra must have no suspicions that anyone was in her den. They'd discussed how to pass the time. Stakeouts were boring at the best of times, this one even more so. Could they have music? They decided they could, but only one at a time with in-the-ear earplugs, no sound spillage. They'd tested them beforehand, fixing a maximum volume. Hayley and Fayyad both had tablets, so could read or watch a film. Reception was too poor for TV, though texts and emails were OK. One of them would be on duty at all times, allowed no electronic distraction. They'd fixed on half-hour watches. Chat was to be at an absolute minimum, Chitra could come anytime, and if she heard, saw or smelt anything unusual she would fly. And most likely escape, as she knew the cemetery far better than they did.

It was Fayyad's turn on watch, he had the lit torch on his lap. Their chairs were at the rear, close to the wall, so they would have nothing to stumble over when Chitra came and the lights were out. Hayley was reading; he could see her face in the light of her tablet. He was impressed how she was able to switch off, to concentrate when needs be. Her martial arts training perhaps.

It was stuffy. A constable had bricked them in, so if Chitra came from round the back for any reason she wouldn't see a hole in the wall. Sufficient air leaked in to breathe, but two people inside made the atmosphere hot and fuggy. They'd have to live with it, and hope she wouldn't be that long.

There were three coffins, the highest two at shoulder height. The lower one, they'd looked in when he and Jack first entered. It was packed with Chitra's gear, her wardrobe so to speak. There must have been a body in it at one time, so presumably one of the other two coffins now had two bodies in. He shivered at the thought. As a child, it had been a nightmare of his, being chased by gangly skeletons.

Fayyad would have liked to talk, talk was comforting, but it was forbidden, only in emergencies. Hayley was comfortable, absorbed in her reading. How long would he last here on his own, without light or a tablet? In the dark with nothing but his imagination. Not very long, he was sure. He couldn't take total darkness. It was formless, timeless, leaving him nothing to attach himself to. Except skeletons in a box.

This would be his Room 101. Alone in complete blackness with shelves of coffins.

Fayyad ate an energy bar. He didn't like them, hadn't really wanted it. They were too sweet. How dare they call them energy bars! A few grains packed into a gummy sugar paste. He swilled his mouth out with water, wetted a tissue and dabbed his face.

Breathe easily, listen. Nothing but a faint buzzing in his ears, which presumably was always there but he never heard. The sounds of the cemetery were shut out by the mausoleum walls. There might be an owl, aircraft overhead, distant traffic, the trains out to Southend, in to Liverpool Street; none of it penetrated. They were in a cave, and should be wearing bearskins, speaking in grunts round a smoky fire.

He tiptoed to the door and put his ear to it, not expecting to hear anything. Was that a train? Maybe. When he turned round, Hayley was watching him. She smiled. He gave a silent sigh, rolling his eyes. She nodded in sympathy.

Still on his feet, he examined the urn behind their chairs. Sort of Greek, with two large handles. Jack had put a hand in, and shown him the grey dust. One of the Baron family who had died 120 years ago. Fayyad had never been frightened of ashes. That was just powder. Skeletons were the fear, grinning skulls, clawing fingers. Two boxes of them on either side, plotting when to pounce.

So juvenile.

Where did Chitra go to the toilet? There was one at the side of the office building, left open for them. But what a chore it would be to use it. They'd have to take out the stones to get out. Go, and somehow put the stones back again, from the inside. He'd try to hold out. Pissing in a pot wouldn't work. Chitra would smell it instantly. She must have a key to the toilet, he thought. Though Jack had told him she could pick locks.

Hayley was tapping him on the wrists and pointing to her watch. He nodded gratefully, his shift was up. He had half an hour to indulge himself. He passed her the torch. She turned off her tablet. He turned his on.

An email had come in from Jack. He read:
I know why she was killed up there.
Fayyad emailed back:
Why?

And waited impatiently for a reply. He looked at his other emails, answered a couple, texted his wife. And then the email came from Jack:

Meet me when you're done.

He was annoyed, stuck in this damned box, and Jack being cryptic. He emailed to him:

Why can't you tell me?

Another wait. Reception was down to one stripe. He rose and moved around the room. At the door, reception picked up. He glanced over to Hayley. She was sitting still, watching him at the door.

Jack's reply came:

I can't write it all out. Too complicated. I'm on the Flats with my telescope. The moon's good, Mars is there. Phone me when you're done. We'll meet up and talk.

Fayyad realised he would get no more.

Chapter 51

Chitra was strolling down Sebert Road towards the cemetery. If anyone was coming towards her, she'd cross over. She didn't trust men this time of night. No, she didn't trust men anytime. That builder had been all right, but it was best to avoid them all. She was most likely a lesbian. Maybe a lesbian group would help with her housing. She couldn't go on climbing into the cemetery every night.

With her new found wealth, she'd bought a puffer jacket at Peacocks in Westfield shopping centre, then gone to their washrooms and had as full a wash as she could in a public toilet. She needed a shower. The only ones she knew that were free were in community centres, and the people there were nosy. Tomorrow, she'd go to the Atherton Leisure Centre, shower, wash her hair, have a good body scrub. And then go for a swim.

Earlier that evening, she'd gone to the Picture House cinema. She'd loaded herself up with sweets and a tub of popcorn, and sat in the front row, legs stretched out, munching. Chitra hadn't known what was on beforehand, so settled for the first one starting in the four-screen cinema. One of the Bourne series. Lots of chases and shootouts, Matt Damon and a girl. Some shady people wanted to kill him and he had to get them first.

Earlier in the afternoon, she'd spent a few hours trying to find a place to live. All the agencies wanted ID. She didn't have any, and if she had, she'd be seen to be too young. Having money wasn't enough. A Pakistani man offered her a room, but she didn't trust him. Besides, it was only in a family house. They'd ask too many questions, interfere with her comings and goings. She'd tried a four star hotel. ID wanted. Three star, ditto. She could try one of those places on the Romford Road, full of prostitutes and business men. They wouldn't care, if she paid cash in advance. Really, she needed to age up, buy some make-up and a wig, stuff her bra and wear a short skirt. But the police might take her in, or she'd be grabbed by a pimp. That was why she wanted to get into one of the good hotels. They were safe and private, but they wanted IDs. The ones that didn't were seedy and dangerous.

She'd have to steal some ID.

Chitra was passing Mia's house, opposite the infant school. A light was on upstairs, but Mia's room, she knew, was at the back overlooking the garden. She'd contact her, maybe this weekend. Take her out for a coffee and a chat. Chitra would have to phone her as she'd thrown her old phone away. People kept trying to contact her. Whenever she looked there were missed calls, texts from the cops asking her to phone for her own safety. Didn't they realise they were the last people she'd contact? In next to no time, she'd be bustled along to a gaggle of social workers, who would decide her life for her. Maybe send her home. What did they know about her family life? They'd believe her mum and stepdad. The pig.

The mausoleum had been good for her. She enjoyed the way she didn't give a damn about corpses in coffins. They were dead, fully dead. Just bones and rags. Why let that worry you, when live human beings were the danger? But the sneaking about, leaving before anyone was in work, that wore her down, and not coming back till after dark. At least no one lived in the cemetery, so once in, she had it all to herself.

But its time had ended. She must move on.

Chitra was at the gate. This was the tricky part. It was only just after eleven, so there were people still around. She had to pick her moment and get in sharp. She laid her back-pack down and watched the traffic. There wasn't much, but being at the end of the road, headlights could pick her out. A car was coming, lights glaring. She darted into the shadows at the side, and waited until it had gone. Nothing coming. Quickly, she opened the gate and slipped inside.

Chitra drew into the shrubbery, where she crouched for half a minute, peering out. No one had seen her. Keeping to one side, she went further in, safer with each step as darkness enclosed her. A fox crossed ahead. She'd seen it before and wondered where its hole was. Did it have a family? It was gone in the gloom. A bat flew overhead, a glimmer and it was lost.

She went into the toilet by the office. Chitra had a key but found it was open tonight. Careless of them, but they were careless. When she'd first come, she'd been able to get into the office by a back window. And found a key to the key rack in a drawer. People are so stupid. It was then she'd taken the keys to the mausoleum and to the toilet.

She flushed the toilet. The nearest houses were too far away to hear, but she kept the light off. That might be seen. She brushed her teeth and washed. There were paper towels; normally she'd take hers away with her, but there were a few in the bin, so she threw her own in too.

Tomorrow, get ID. Always good to have something set to do. For an Asian girl of about nineteen, two years older than her actual age. The University of East London would be a good bet. Students were sloppy with their gear. Using it, she could stay in a half decent hotel and look for a permanent room. Try some lesbian websites. Perhaps get a bank account, though the owner of the ID would already have one. But then why not have another? People do have two. She had money; it wasn't as if she was going to rob a bank.

Money eased your life.

She crossed the tarmac, over to the mausoleum. Her little house, her home. Everyone else was afraid to go in there. Spooked. She took out the keys, she always had trouble with the key in the dark, finding the keyhole. What was that? She'd heard something.

Chitra listened intently. An owl hooted from the trees. No sound from inside. There were no ghosts. She turned the key in the lock. It was a good thing she'd greased it and oiled the hinges. The first time, it had been so stiff, she'd had trouble getting in, but then no one had been inside for a hundred and twenty years.

And, after her, likely they wouldn't for another hundred and twenty.

Chitra stepped in, closing the door behind her. And was blinded by a light. She put her hands to her face as strong arms grasped her. She bit, scratched, stamped and yelled as she was thrown into a half nelson.

'Let me go!'

Her wrists were snapped into handcuffs.

Chapter 52

Jack had set up his telescope on the Flats. He was more or less in the middle, on level ground, away from trees, as far away from street lighting and houses as he could get. It was a walk of several hundred yards from the car park, and so he'd used his wheelbarrow to carry the telescope, mount and battery. He'd picked the barrow up earlier from his lockup as the one usually in the van was still held by the police along with his bricklaying tools.

He could, if he had to, manage without a wheelbarrow, hump it all, taking it slow. Better when Mia was with him; she'd take the mount, but he had the wheelbarrow, so why not use it? You only have one back. Builders too often take chances, working lives cut short by back trouble. More of a problem when you work on your own. He'd learnt, after a few accidents, to minimise risks.

He felt free here, alone. Relaxed. This was his element. Around the horizon was a circle of light spilling into the sky from houses, traffic and streetlights. Useless to observe at that level. Best was overhead, least light polluted. Tonight, there was a half moon, washed by smoky clouds, but overhead was relatively clear. He'd seen from his astronomy magazine that M31, the Andromeda Galaxy, was high in the east.

Knowing where to look, he started from the Square of Pegasus. That big, welcoming square, which Mia said was like a kid's drawing of a horse's body. You followed where its neck would be, which was the constellation of Andromeda. Two stars along from the corner star of Pegasus, then two up, and somewhere around there was M31.

It was the only object that could be seen outside our galaxy, the Milky Way, with the naked eye. Not that Jack had ever seen it without an instrument. As a smudge through binoculars, and often as a bigger smudge through his telescope. But tonight it was almost overhead, the best possible place to minimise pollution.

By eye at first, and then with his finderscope, the small low-powered telescope on the barrel of the main one, he turned his telescope to the area of sky. And then he looked through the main instrument. That always threw him, the shock in the change of magnification. Easy to be confused at what you were looking at with so many more stars visible.

He thought he had it. And took out the eye-piece and switched it for his most powerful. The Andromeda Galaxy was there, blurry, but there. He twisted the focus gently to and fro. That was pretty good. An oval sweep, a glowing beret, two and half million light years away. Which meant he was seeing it as it had been two and half million years ago. It was possible the Andromeda Galaxy had exploded, and was gone. Not likely, but in the realms of possibility. He marvelled at the time and distance. He'd try a photo with his phone... Amateurish, but worth a go.

'Hello, Jack.'

He was thrown, out of the stars, and into the world. A human voice. He withdrew from the scope.

It was Maria. He couldn't see her face, but the outline of her body, her hair.

'It was hard to find you,' she said.

'How did you know I was here?'

'Beryl told me.'

'Ah,' he said. 'She's poly, you know.' He was showing off his new vocabulary.

'I did know,' she said. 'She was locked out, and you got her in.'

'I did.'

'Anything else?'

'Like what?' he said innocently.

'Like the things poly people do.'

'Would it matter?'

There was a long pause. She was about a metre away. A spectre.

'I thought I could be poly,' she said. 'Then I found I couldn't. I'm not saying it's a bad thing. It's just that I couldn't keep switching. I get attached.'

'I know what you mean,' he said. 'I'm too old. Which is probably a sad thing to say. Or maybe sadder to admit. Or maybe it isn't. Do you want to see the Andromeda Galaxy?'

'Yes, I would like that.'

She came to the telescope.

'It's the farthermost thing that can be seen with the naked eye. The only one outside our galaxy.'

'What about the Magellanic Clouds?'

'I forgot about those. But are they outside the Milky Way?'

'Sort of satellites to it,' she said. 'They can only be seen in the southern hemisphere. I read that in your astronomy magazine. I can't see through the eyepiece if you have your arm round me.'

'M31 is not going anywhere,' he said.

And kissed her.

It was a long embrace. Admitting they weren't poly. With some relief. Melding in the darkness, lips seeking lips, hands pressing, in the very centre of Wanstead Flats. A hunger for recognition, to be known. A patching up of old quarrels with the salve of presence. All done, all over, forgiven.

'Might I see the Andromeda galaxy now?'

They detached. And she looked through the eyepiece.

'Oh, it's good,' she said. 'A bit bleary, but for London, that's magnificent. I think I can see a spiral arm. Or is that just because I want to? I'm going to take a photo.'

He gave her some space, and his phone rang. It was Fayyad.

'Hello, Jack. I'm at the car park in the middle of the Flats. Where are you?'

'I'll shine my torch,' he said. 'A few hundred yards east of you...' He took his torch out of the wheelbarrow and shone it in the sky, a long bright beam. 'Can you see it?'

'Yes. I'll head that way. See you in a couple of minutes. Keep shining.'

He rang off.

'Who was that?' she said.

'A copper.'

'A strange place to meet a copper.'

'He's a friend.'

'Just a friend?'

'I told you I'm not poly, or bi for that matter. I've some information for him. I told him I'd be here.'

'I'd best be off then.'

'You don't have to go.' Though he wondered how he could deal with them both.

'I'll go.' She pressed a finger to his lips. He held it there.

'Come to my place tomorrow,' he said.

'I will,' she said. 'I'll bring some food. About eight.'

She drew away. His arm yearned after her. She was walking off. He could just see her, heading through the gorse, down a path. And then lost sight of her in the darkness of the heath.

A second chance. Both a little wiser. He was impressed with her knowing about the Magellanic Clouds. Looks and rapport.

'Hello, Jack.'

Jack swung the torch and caught Fayyad a little way off, approaching him.

Chapter 53

They packed up the telescope together, wrapping the body in the plastic sheet. They put the telescope, mount and battery in the wheelbarrow and headed for the car park, Jack pushing the barrow, Fayyad by his side.

'We caught Chitra,' he said. 'She fought like a wild cat. I don't like handcuffing juveniles but she didn't give us any choice. She's now in the custody suite, spitting and snapping at whoever comes near. We'll interview her in the morning.' He stopped. 'I needn't have come here to tell you that. But you've got something for me.'

'I have,' said Jack. 'I've been puzzling why Kim was killed at my site. I couldn't make sense of it. And then it came to me when I was unwrapping my telescope this evening. I put plastic round it for protection when I cart it about. It struck me; Kim needed protection.'

'Sure she did, but how's plastic sheet going to help?'

'Coe had left her counting the money. Ten thousand quid in a canvas bag. She counts it, all correct, and leaves the office, but where is she to go? She could come back to my place, could go to her mother's. Either way, she doesn't want to walk the streets with ten thousand pounds in a bag.'

'At half two in the morning. Not advisable.'

'So she needs to hide it somewhere. And it's only in a canvas bag. The money would get soaked if she left it in the open. She can't leave it in the office. The cleaner or Maureen would find it in the morning. She can't put it in the flower hut, not without risk of her mother discovering it. So she looks about the cemetery. Somewhere to hide the money, keep it dry, until she can pick it up in the morning. And she comes across my site.'

'The plastic sheet,' exclaimed Fayyad.

'Precisely. The concrete footings were covered with a large plastic sheet to keep any rain off,' went on Jack. 'She could leave it under there. Well under. That would keep the contents dry and out of sight. She could then come back to my place. Leave with me in the morning. And while I'm getting my tools out of the van, retrieve the bag.'

'I'm with you so far. She's at the site on her own, doesn't want to cart the cash through the streets, so hides it under your plastic sheet. Then someone must have come. Saul coming back, changing his mind?'

'No. Not him. He's gone home to his wife. Someone else. Who lives in the cemetery. Someone who'd run off when I came looking for my daughter...'

'Chitra.'

'I arrived in my van and caught Mia climbing over the gate. Chitra was already over and runs off. I go off with Mia in my van. That's all I can manage. All I care about when it comes to it. But Chitra didn't go far. She watched me leave and then went back to the cemetery. She climbed the gate and was heading for her mausoleum when she saw Kim, probably heard her first, and investigated. And saw her hiding a bag under a plastic sheet. She waited until Kim left and got the bag. Amazingly, it was full of bank notes.'

'So we've got Chitra and the money. We haven't got a dead body.'

'Kim must've returned for some reason. Maybe she heard something, maybe she changed her mind about leaving the cash. We'll never know which. But she sees Chitra. And they fight over the bag. A desperate fight. Kim so badly wanted that money, so too did Chitra. Chitra had a knife, one she'd taken from Alison's kitchen. Kim was overpowering her, so she stabbed her. Took the cash and her necklace, and went home.'

Jack had finished his tale. Fayyad was silent for a while.

'It fits,' he said. Then added as an afterthought, 'But we found Saul's pen there.'

'A detail. Chitra had four hours until daylight. She had the pen already, must have taken it some other time, and so goes back to the site and drops it to implicate Coe.'

'It worked,' said Fayyad.

They were at the van in the car park. Fayyad's car was parked alongside.

'I wasn't happy with Coe as the killer,' said Fayyad. 'Why would he kill her at your site? We know he went back to his wife... And why not take back the cash if he'd killed Kim? But Chitra. It fits. The cash, the necklace, the knife.' He laughed mirthlessly. 'This throws it all up in the air. Catch the pieces coming down. There'll be fun in the morning. Release Coe, interview Chitra.'

Jack had unlocked his van and was loading the telescope mount in.

'If she wasn't such a thief,' he said, 'the money, the necklace...'

'Then she wouldn't have killed in the first place.' Fayyad patted Jack on the shoulder. 'Thanks, Jack. It was worth a midnight stroll on the Flats. But I must get home, I have to be up early in the morning and put the boss in the picture.'

'What will happen to her?'

Fayyad shrugged. 'It's murder. No way round that.'

'But she's a kid, just 17. Had a rotten life. Abused at home, no help from the authorities...'

'You know what she did, Jack.'

'I do. But she wasn't out to kill, a kid with every disadvantage...'

Fayyad shrugged. 'A good lawyer could get that taken into consideration. But I can't see her going down for less than ten years. From then on, it depends how she is in prison. If she goes around knifing fellow inmates...'

'And if she's a model prisoner, gets herself educated?'

Fayyad shrugged. 'I'm not the Parole Board, Jack. You're asking me questions I can't answer. Chitra killed a woman. That's the nub of it. She'll go to jail. A young offenders' unit till she's 18, then prison. How she gets on inside depends on her. I hope she wises up... But we get no say in the matter.' He began walking off. 'Must get home. Too much to do in the morning.'

Chapter 54

Jack parked outside the cemetery. Last night, he'd been home by one and had slept fairly well, woken by the alarm. He'd had scrambled egg on toast for breakfast and made cheese sandwiches for lunch. When making tea, he made sure he had enough to fill his thermos.

So efficient this morning.

He hoped the cops had finished with his site, so he could get working. But first, as promised, he'd mortar in the stones of the mausoleum back wall. Then put in his invoice. You never know with authorities, how long they might take to pay you. Though it would come in the end.

Fayyad had had less sleep than he had, Jack was sure. He had to be in the same time as his boss. How had she taken the new tale? Sometimes an old idea is hard to shift. You get locked in. Like the Vatican ridiculing Galileo when he said the Earth went round the Sun.

Not that he didn't have his own prejudices, not being as young as he was. Well, a 13 year old daughter revealed that. And all these sexual ideas with new labels but not new at all. The Romans had tried everything going.

Maria was coming over tonight. They had a lot to talk about. Might work this time, might bust up in a couple of weeks. Had she got a good picture of the Andromeda Galaxy? His own wasn't up to much.

Something to look forward to.

He took his wheelbarrow out of the van. Bricklaying gear, first for the mausoleum and then for the site where, hopefully, he could get on with building the wall. He suddenly recalled, the cops still had his long spirit level, float, trowel and line. All taken as part of the crime scene.

How long before he got that lot back? Fayyad had said he owed him one. Well, get my tools back, mate. But for now, what did he have? Jack scrabbled about in the van and withdrew a bucket, a twenty-four inch spirit level, some bricklaying pins, string he could make into a line, a spade and a trowel. He could get by with that. A shovel would be better than a spade, but it would serve. He didn't have a board to make his mortar on, but maybe they'd left that behind; it wouldn't fit in a plastic bag.

Thermos and sandwiches. Mustn't forget those. Too far to trek back to the van for a cup of tea and a snack.

Jack locked up and pushed the barrow through the gates. Instantly, he saw that his first job was a non-starter. Up ahead were police vehicles. The mausoleum was surrounded by crime scene tape. He laughed at the thought that he'd put himself out of work once more. But it did mean Fayyad's boss had taken on board the new narrative.

Postpone that job, until the tape comes off.

Just before the mausoleum, Ruth was at the flower stall. She was having a yellow day. A yellow dress, short sleeved revealing her freckled arms, a yellow peasant like headscarf, yellow flats.

She indicated the mausoleum. 'Maureen says you're responsible for that.'

'I noticed it was being lived in,' he said.

'You do keep your eyes open,' she said. 'Who lived there?'

'A young girl with nowhere to go.'

'But a mausoleum! Under our noses. For how long?'

He shrugged. 'Some time.'

She shook her head. 'They went in first thing with their tape. Before I got here. Had the key. And Saul's back. Two nights they held him. Sarah was worried sick. She doesn't need that, not in her condition. He's in the office. All he said was they'd got it all wrong. Won't say any more than that. Always the way with Saul. He'll tell you as little as possible. But you know some of what's going on. Maureen said you were looking at an old volume yesterday and phoned the cops. How come you know so much?'

'I just saw the hinges had been oiled,' he said, not wanting to go into details.

'Now they've let Saul go, they must think the girl is the killer.'

'What makes you say that?' Curious as to how she'd worked it out.

'Jack, oh Jack, you don't say much but there's a lot ticking up there.' She tapped her temple. 'But even I know they don't send in a crime scene team for a squatter.'

'You're not just a pretty face yourself,' he said with a grin.

Ruth laughed. 'Oh, thank you, young man. True or not, it's the sort of small thing that makes my morning.'

Jack indicated up ahead. 'Now they're done down here, I wonder whether they're off our site.'

'Might be.' And then she came in closer. 'I was thinking about the memorial. Maybe it should be a joint one, for my husband and for Kim. What do you think?'

'A good idea,' he said. 'Both family.'

'Exactly my thought. When you've finished the work, I thought we could have a remembrance ceremony in the hall for the two of them. And when it's over, all come out together and officially unveil the memorial. You'll come, won't you, Jack?'

'Of course. In my best suit.' His only suit. 'I'll go and have a look up top. See if I can get going again.'

He pushed on with the wheelbarrow as far as the mausoleum. Just inside the tape was the policeman he'd spoken to yesterday.

'Hello,' said Jack. 'You lot are busy.'

'I don't know what's going on this morning,' said the constable, flapping a hand. 'First it's up there, then it's down here. Someone's been living here, would you believe, up to something. That's all I know. They don't tell us constables much.' He smiled in exasperation.

Jack could've put him wise, but it wasn't his place. He peered into the mausoleum. The door had been taken off the hinges and leaned against the wall. Inside was fiercely lit and he could see a couple of people in white coveralls, one crawling about the floor, the other doing something to the back wall.

'How about up top?' he said. 'Is that free yet?'

'All done with. I took away the tape first thing. You can get on with your work.'

'Thanks,' said Jack, not mentioning that he'd hoped to be working at the mausoleum too. Plenty of time to do that. The main job was up top. He could do this one whenever they finished. Wouldn't be long, surely? The mausoleum was small.

He continued on his way. Half a dozen cars were outside the crematorium, floral tributes against the wall. They never ceased, one after another, the dead and the grieving. A wreath said SON. That was sad. A motor accident, he guessed. Old people you expected to die. They'd had their time, but a son or daughter was a shock. He thought of Mia and how it would hurt him.

Jack pushed on down the side road, where conkers and leaves had fallen in the night. It seemed to go on forever, but of course it wouldn't. A squirrel raced across at his approach and up a tree. He parked the barrow by his pile of bricks. The tape had gone as the constable had said. It was his space again. Short of tools, but he could work.

Perhaps Chitra had hidden behind these bricks watching Kim. Jack had let her go at Alison's, sympathising with a girl who'd fled home, too young to work, needing money to survive. The victim and the murderer had that in common. Kim was greedy about money. He could imagine the two of them fighting in the dark. Neither would give in. Maybe Kim had got hold of the bag, and Chitra in desperation stabbed her for it.

And the necklace, which she must have taken off the body. That little bit of extra greed. She was a kid, and wanted nice things. She'd never had any, other than those she stole.

He had sympathy, one way and another, for both women, fighting over the money. For the kid who was going to jail for ten years or more. Murder is murder, as Fayyad had said over the Flats. And Kim, poor Kim, with plans for a coffee bar-cum-art gallery, almost divorced from her husband. Just a week or two to go. But he wouldn't get the house, she'd seen to that. And brother-in-law Keith would get evicted when Battersea Dogs & Cats Home came calling.

Jack began loading bricks into the wheelbarrow.

And himself, he recalled. Some time or other, he'd get his share, once the will was sorted, the addition Kim had made on seeing his kitchen. Enough for a dishwasher.

Thank you!

I am grateful to every reader who finishes one of my novels. I have taken you on a journey which I hope you have enjoyed. There are plenty of things you could have been doing, other than reading this book. So, thank you for your time.

If you liked Jack At Death's Door, here's what you can do next:

I'd appreciate a review on Amazon. In that way, you can help me tell other readers about my books. Without reviews authors get few sales on Amazon. So I'd be grateful for your review to help this series get on the move.

You can get a FREE ebook of Jack of Spades if you sign up for my readers' list. You may give it to a friend if you wish. Every month a lucky reader from the list will be sent a free, signed paperback of their choice from the series. Sign up using this link:

http://eepurl.com/buAh5H

When you sign up for my readers' list you will receive my regular newsletter. This will give you news about me, what I'm reading, tell you about my future books, PLUS a variety of giveaways.

Books by DH Smith

DH Smith is the name I use for my Jack of All Trades series. The books are all standalone novels and can be read in any order.

Out Now:
- Jack of All Trades
- Jack of Spades
- Jack o'Lantern
- Jack By The Hedge
- Jack In The Box
- Jack On The Tower
- Jack Recalled
- Jack at Death's Door

Coming Soon:
- Jack at the Gate

Books by Derek Smith

All my books, other than the Jack of All Trades series, are written under the name Derek Smith.

Mystery/Crime
Murder at Any Price

Fantasy
Hell's Chimney
The Prince's Shadow
Elektra

Other
Strikers of Hanbury Street (short stories)
Catching Up (poetry)

Young Adult Novels
Hard Cash
Half a Bike
Fast Food
Frances Fairweather Demon Striker!

Children's Novels
The Good Wolf
Feather Brains
Baker's Boy

For Younger Children
The Magical World of Lucy-Anne
Lucy-Anne's Changing Ways
Jack's Bus

About the Author

I live in Forest Gate in the East End of London. In my working life, I have been a plastics chemist, a gardener and a stage manager before becoming a professional writer. I began with plays, working with several theatre companies, and had a few plays on radio and TV, as well as on the stage. In the early 80s I became involved in running a co-operative bookshop and vegetarian café in Stratford, learning to cook, and having my first go at writing a novel. The first was a mess, and, after too many rewrites, binned. The transition from drama to novels took me a couple of years to get to grips with. My first success was a young adult novel, Hard Cash, published by Faber. Buoyed up by this, I stuck with children's work, did school visits, and made a hand to mouth living as a full time author, topped up with some evening class work in creative writing at City University and the Mary Ward Centre in Holborn. A few adult fiction titles appeared from time to time, between the children's list, and I have since been working more in that direction with my Jack of All Trades series.

My full name is Derek Howard Smith. I write as DH Smith for my Jack of All Trades series; all other books appear under Derek Smith. Earlham Books is my own imprint.

www.dereksmithwriter.com

9 781909 804302